What Happens in Vegas

SHANA GRAY

HEADLINE
ETERNAL

The right of Shana Gray to be identified as the Author of
the Work has been asserted by her in accordance with the
Copyright, Designs and Patents Act 1988.

First published in Great Britain in 2018
by HEADLINE ETERNAL
An imprint of HEADLINE PUBLISHING GROUP

1

Cataloguing in Publication Data is available from the British Library

ISBN 978 1 4722 6001 7

Typeset in 11/14 pt Minion Pro by Jouve (UK), Milton Keynes

Printed and bound in Great Britain by CPI Group (UK) Ltd, Croydon, CR0 4YY

Headline's policy is to use papers that are natural, renewable and recyclable
products and made from wood grown in well-managed forests and other
controlled sources. The logging and manufacturing processes are expected to
conform to the environmental regulations of the country of origin.

HEADLINE PUBLISHING GROUP
An Hachette UK Company
Carmelite House
50 Victoria Embankment
London EC4Y 0DZ

www.headlineeternal.com
www.headline.co.uk
www.hachette.co.uk

I went to London, England, this past February for a reader conference. One of the highlights was meeting my UK editor Kate Bryne. For the past two years, and during Working Girl, all our communication has been by email. So, finally being able to meet in person was fantastic. She and Emily Gowers made me feel like a superstar with books and stickers to sign in the Headline office. That was so cool!

We have a rather unique connection too – Swansea, Wales, and one day perhaps we can walk along the Mumbles. Kate, you've been so amazingly supportive, and spending time with you in London was simply wonderful. Thank you for believing in me and GWA. This book is for you. xo

Acknowledgments

The idea for this series came to me in the summer of 2017. I was inspired to create a fun Girls' Weekend Away story, where girl-friends reunite for some crazy-good times, bonding, and shenanigans. Of course, meeting a man along the way to complicate things was a MUST.

Helping me bring this story to life are three very important people and I send out my thanks and a full heart to you all – Louise – you are the BEST! You always know what to say to keep me sane, Kristin – I love your sparkly unicorn, and Kate – if you hadn't fallen in love with my idea, well there would be no Girls' Weekend Away series. Behind the scenes are so many people that all deserve a shout out, the cover designers, marketers, copy editors, and everyone else that touched this book . . . my heartfelt thanks.

So, off we go to Vegas and begin the stories of Bonni, Celia, Ava and Fredi. Let the Shenanigans begin! xo

What Happens in Vegas

Chapter 1

From: **Bonni Connolly <bonni@iphone.ca>**
Date: Thu, Jan 11, 2018 at 16:09
Subject: Fwd: Check Out This Great Offer!
To: **Ava, Celia, Fredi**

See below. My latest case has been kicking my ass and I could use some downtime. And who better to tackle Sin City with than my girls? VEGAS, BABY! Who's in?
Bons

---------- Forwarded message ----------

To: **Bonni Connolly**
From: **Gladiators Casino & Resort Hotel**
<deals@gladiatorcasinoresort.com>
Date: Wed, Jan 10, 2018 at 9:17
Subject: Check Out This Great Offer!

Promotional pricing for the newest hotel on the Vegas Strip

**Book a room now for $49 a night
(minimum 3-night stay) and get
$100 worth of chips absolutely FREE**

Clink *LINK* to book!

From: **Ava Trent <Ava.Trent@edbridgegroup.com>**
Date: Thu, Jan 11, 2018 at 16:16
Subject: Re: Fwd: Check Out This Great Offer!
To: **Bonni, Celia, Fredi**

Oh my God! I'm in. Just tell me when and I'll clear my calendar. What's more overtime? I basically already sleep here! Looking forward to seeing you ladies!!! <3
Ava XO
Ava Trent, MBA, BComm
Director
Edbridge Group
Cell: 555.447.3200
e-mail: Ava.Trent@edbridgegroup.com

From: **Fredi Cannon <Fredi@delightweddingdesigns.com>**
Date: Thu, Jan 11, 2018 at 16:20
Subject: Re: Fwd: Check Out This Great Offer!
To: **Bonni, Celia, Ava**

I'm free 1st Mar wknd – only avail time. The bridezillas will come after me otherwise. Gladiators, huh? After spending all

my time with emotional women, I'm ready for some beefcake.
xxxxxx
Best,
Fredi
It's Your Day!
Head Designer, Delight Wedding Dresses

From: **Celia <Fox foximom@iphone.com>**
Date: Thu, Jan 11, 2018 at 16:22
Subject: Re: Fwd: Check Out This Great Offer!
To: **Bonni, Ava, Fredi**

Yaaaas!!!! I love my kids, but, God, do I need a weekend away.
First weekend in March works for me. That's supposed to be
Dickhead's week with the kids, but I'll line up my mother as
back-up.

I'm up for anything, so long as we avoid the wedding
chapels! Haha, j/k. #notreally #bringonthetequila
C

From: **Bonni Connolly <bonni@iphone.ca>**
Date: Thu, Jan 11, 2018 at 16:26
Subject: Re: Fwd: Check Out This Great Offer!
To: **Celia, Ava, Fredi**

Fantastic! I'll book two rooms. That gives us a month to save
up our coins for the slot machines! Woohoo, big spenders!

We'll figure out a full itinerary later, but since we need to get
Celia tequila stat, let's meet in the lobby bar, say, noon?
Although it will really be 3 pm for me and Fredi . . .

So pumped! It'll be our own little college reunion, complete with copious amounts of alcohol and Celia probably puking in a bush again . . .
Bons

From: **Fredi Cannon <Fredi@delightweddingdesigns.com>**
Date: Thu, Jan 11, 2018 at 16:29
Subject: Re: Fwd: Check Out This Great Offer!
To: **Bonni, Celia, Ava**

Ugh, yeah, time change is going to take some getting used to. Maybe I'll find a guy who will volunteer to help me over my jet lag, wink wink.

Oh, Lord, I remember the bush. The best, though, was when she puked in the back seat of that fraternity bro's brand-new Beamer. We should start a pool. Where will Celia drunkenly puke on our girls' weekend? xxxxx
Best,
Fredi
It's Your Day!
Head Designer, Delight Wedding Dresses

From: **Ava <Ava.Trent@edbridgegroup.com>**
Date: Thu, Jan 11, 2018 at 16:31
Subject: Re: Fwd: Check Out This Great Offer!
To: **Fredi, Celia, Bonni**

You guys are too much! This is going to be epic and I can't wait! But Celia's a mom now! And Bonni's a cop! It'll be tons of fun, but surely it won't get as crazy as it did in college.
XO

Ava Trent, MBA, BComm
Director
Edbridge Group
Cell: 555.447.3200
e-mail: Ava.Trent@edbridgegroup.com

From: **Celia Fox <foximom@iphone.com>**
Date: Thu, Jan 11, 2018 at 16:32
Subject: Re: Fwd: Check out This Great Offer!
To: **Bonni, Ava, Fredi**

Leave the badge at home, Bon-Bon, and put me down for $20
on some blonde bimbo's stupid designer shoes.
#fml
C

From: **Bonni Connolly <bonni@iphone.ca>**
Date: Thu, Jan 11, 2018 at 16:45
Subject: Re: Fwd: Check Out This Great Offer!
To: **Ava, Celia, Fredi**

This is going to be the best trip ever . . .
Bons

Chapter 2

Bonni found a perfect spot in the bar. She was early, of course, to scope things out and get the lay of the land. Situated in the center of the casino, it was up three steps and gave a good vantage point. She settled in the chair with her back to the decorative wall behind her. A lawman never put his back to the door. It had been ingrained into her; first by her dad when she was a kid and then by her training officer in the police academy. *Always be aware of your surroundings, have a backup plan, and know your escape route.*

Bonni crossed her jean-clad legs and bobbed her booted toe, carefully scanning the crowd on the casino floor. She drew in a deep sigh and closed her eyes as the stress tightening her muscles began to seep out of her. It was a good plan to come to Vegas with her girls. She needed the break after the last few months. Being in Frauds for so long, Bonni would have thought she'd seen it all, and yet . . . How people think they can get away with shit never failed to surprise Bonni. It had taken months to build the case, get enough intel in order to file charges. But enough of work. She was done for the next few days and excited to begin the shenanigans. Bonni leaned back and draped her arms along the cushioned backs of the chairs next to her. Now all she needed was a drink.

The bar wasn't crowded yet, but then it was what . . . she looked at her Apple watch, just about noon here and 3 p.m. at home. A very hunky waiter, decked out in gladiator garb, complete with a gold warrior skirt slung low on his hips, approached her. *My, my, my, so there were gladiators here, after all.*

'Can I get you anything?' he asked. His voice was low, syrupy with a slight accent, and Bonni suspected he put it on for more tips, or similar 'aren't I dreamy?' scenarios. No, knock it off. She was determined to do her best not to look beyond the surface of things while she was on vacation. She needed to rein in her tendency to be suspicious.

She returned his smile. 'An Old-fashioned would be great, thank you very much.'

The view of his leaving was just as nice as the view of his arrival. Bonni let her gaze linger on his powerful back. It had been far too long since she'd run her fingers over a man's muscles.

Maybe she could talk the girls into getting tickets for the *Thunder Down Under* show, and made a mental note to suggest it. Sometimes a feast for the eyes could be almost as satisfying as . . . nope, who was she kidding? Physical and visual were a chasm apart.

Female voices and happy squeals rose above the sounds of the casino. Bonni bolted to her feet, knowing it had to be her crew. Her three friends exploded up the steps into the circular Coliseum bar, and Bonni's face split with a wide smile.

'God! I can't believe we're all finally together again!' Fredi tossed her handbag on to a chair.

Celia opened her arms and Bonni fell into her hug.

'Come on, girls, I need hugs. Hugs, hugs, hugs – it's been way too long.'

Bonni heard the emotion in Celia's voice and it struck a chord deep inside her. She had to fight back the gush of sentimentality that came rushing.

'Oh, it has been soooo long!' Ava cried. She and Fredi smooshed into the group hug.

Bonni felt like she'd come home. Home to her girls. Home to the safety of her soul sisters. The group had been inseparable through college and then they had been separated by life, but they had kept in touch religiously through the years. This was the first time they'd all been together since Celia's wedding, together once again in a big, sloppy, emotional reunion smack dab in the middle of the bar. Ava had tears in her eyes, and Bonni smoothed her hand over Ava's silky, dark hair. 'Honey, it's all good. We're here together.'

'I know,' Ava sniffed – she was the romantic and the most sentimental of the bunch. 'I'm just so happy. You know me and happy tears.'

Fredi was the first to disengage. She was like that, not normally a big fan of public displays of affection, although every now and then you might get a bit of a squishy hug out of her. 'Okay, girls, have you checked out the dudes in this place? There is some seriously hot eye candy around here. We are going to have some fun.' She ran from one sentence to another in a rush. Sometimes it was hard keeping her on track. Her eyes were full of enthusiasm and her dramatic eye make-up made the crystal blue of her irises seem almost translucent.

Celia waggled her finger at her. 'Come on now. This is a girls' weekend. It's not for boys. Well, you guys might want to have a quick fling or a one-night stand or something, but not me.' She threw her hands in the air. 'I'm done with that.'

Ava rubbed Celia's back as they followed Bonni to the group of chairs she'd claimed. 'Now listen to me,' she said, 'there is hope for you yet. Don't be a man-hater. Just because you met a dick who put two babies in your belly before walking away, it doesn't mean all men are assholes.'

Celia flopped down on one of the low chairs and crossed her long, elegant legs. You wouldn't know she had two kids and was a stay-at-home mom, who struggled to keep things afloat by writing greeting cards and magazine articles. She was classy, cool and looked like she had it all together. Bonni always wondered how Celia managed to stay sane.

'Well,' Celia said, and lifted a delicate shoulder. 'I'm just here for the drinks and you girls. I'm sworn off men for life, and I don't care what any of you say.'

Bonni snorted, and the rest of the girls burst out laughing. 'Likely! We know you have needs, like the rest of us. You just like to hide it and pretend it's a secret.'

Celia raised her nose in the air and tried not to laugh. She leaned forward and crooked her finger. The women leaned in. 'A wise old bird once told me all a girl needs are fresh batteries and good lube,' she whispered, like it was a leaked government secret on WikiLeaks.

They burst into gales of laughter, which attracted glances from the other bar patrons.

'Well, true,' Bonni said. 'But you know we're right.'

'No comment, Ms Cop. I'm not here to be interrogated by you. I know what I know.' Celia flicked a long California-blonde strand of hair over her shoulder and turned her sea-green eyes on Bonni.

Fredi stood and walked to the faux stone half-wall that ringed the bar. She was the stunning one. She was a Carrie Bradshaw lookalike: petite, beautiful, with classic features, killer legs and body, and long, flowing, curly locks she could do whatever she liked with. Only she was way more gorgeous than Carrie Bradshaw. She was a fashionista too, and not afraid to experiment with her clothes. Bonni envied that. She glanced down at her ordinary jeans, her leather ankle boots, and rubbed her palms on her thighs. She was not the kind of person to sacrifice comfort for fashion, especially after traveling for more than half a day!

Fredi spun around, her hair bouncing in a chaos of curls and her green eyes sparkling, then loped back to the seats and flopped down, announcing, 'We are going to have some fun! This place is rocking. How amazingly cool we're here during its opening. There'll be all kinds of specials.'

She and Bonni were the thrifty ones.

Celia scooted forward on her seat as if she had some great secret to tell. 'So, how wild do we want to get this weekend?'

Bonni smiled and Fredi jumped in her seat. Ava gave Celia a quizzical look. 'What exactly do you have in mind?' she asked. 'Don't forget, you're a mom and sworn off men.'

Celia flipped her the bird and had just opened her mouth to reply when she froze, her mouth dropped open at something she'd seen behind their group.

'OMG, guys!' Celia's eyes were nearly popping out of her head.

Bonni saw what had caught Celia's attention. Her gladiator waiter was approaching with her drink on his tray. *Wait till the girls get a load of him*, she thought, and waited to see their reactions.

'Ladies.' His deep voice had Ava and Fredi spinning in their seats. Their jaws dropped in unison. Bonni smiled and bit back laughter. They'd just met their first gladiator. Promise kept! 'Welcome to the Coliseum. We're very happy you chose us for your Las Vegas vacation,' he said to the women, as he bent down to put Bonni's drink on a coaster that resembled a Roman shield and flashed them a sexy grin. 'Are you ready for some drinks?' He stood back, his stance clearly practiced, muscled legs wide, powerful arms crossed, and tray tucked at his side.

Her friends stumbled over each other to speak and it came out as a big, sloppy mess. He smiled and dimples peeked in his cheeks. Bonni glanced at Celia. She thought she might have to reach over and push her mouth closed. She was fairly drooling. So much for not being interested in men.

Bonni reached for her Old-fashioned and sipped, watching the girls order their drinks while flirting outrageously with the waiter. When he turned and walked away they fell silent and did the exact same thing Bonni had: watch him with tongues lolling. Then they all looked at each other and gave a little squeal.

'Holy cow, did you ever pick the right hotel, Bonni!' Ava nodded with approval

Bonni shrugged her shoulders. 'It was all about timing. The email arrived, I needed a break, and who else was I going to call? I can't believe how long it's been since we've all been close enough for a group hug! And yeah, I think we've got the right hotel.'

Celia sat on the edge of her chair and grabbed the promotional flyer on the table. 'Time to plan what to do. We need to find out what's going on, what we need to see, so we don't miss a thing.'

Fredi rolled her eyes. 'Yes, Mom. Remember: we're not your kids. We don't need you to plan our days on a fridge whiteboard and make sure we have snacks and nap time. We're here to have fun. Take one day at a time and just go with the flow. And maybe live a little bit on the wild side.'

Celia looked at her with sad eyes. 'Go with the flow. I don't even know what that is anymore. My days are so tightly scheduled, I no longer recognize spontaneity.'

'We'll get you back into the swing of things this weekend,' Fredi promised, and reached forward to squeeze Celia's hand.

Celia nodded and chewed her lower lip. 'A man would be a nice diversion too,' she whispered in a low voice.

'You just said you weren't interested. Make up your mind, girl! Why don't you just stick to your batteries and good lube for the time being?' Fredi replied. 'Do you really want to get hooked up with a man again?'

Celia glanced up; she was like an open book and plainly showed her emotion. 'You know, I would. There has to be a good one out there. But –' she paused and nodded before continuing – 'I'm not likely to find him in Vegas. Everyone here just comes for a good time. You know, "what happens in Vegas, stays in Vegas" sort of thing.'

'Okay, how about we chill on the desperately seeking a man situation and focus on the fact that we're here together.' Bonni decided she had to steer the conversation away from the male species; plus, she was hungry. 'I think I'm going to order some food here to tide me over until later. I'm starved. Anyone else?'

'Good idea,' Ava said, 'Some nourishment for the drinking marathon that doth approach.'

'Oh, that's right. Celia's pool is still open. Want to get your bets in before she pukes, ladies?' Fredi asked.

'Okay, look.' Celia gave her a sideways glance. 'Can we at least get one drink under our belts first? Besides, it probably won't take much to get me plastered these days. I haven't tied one on in so long, I don't have any tolerance left.'

'You? No tolerance? Not sure I believe that,' Fredi teased.

'Don't worry,' Bonni assured her. 'We'll hold your hair back.' The women laughed again, and Celia tossed the brochure at Bonni.

'My inevitable drunkenness aside, we should see what shows

are on while we're here. What about that Cirque du Soleil *O*? It's the one that's supposed to be sexy, right?' Celia asked. 'And I could use a bit of sexy right about now.'

'Or *Thunder Down Under*,' Ava suggested. 'Those guys look so hot and, if we're lucky, we might get pulled up on stage for a lap dance or something.' She clapped her hands excitedly.

'I'm down for that.' Fredi smiled and nodded.

'Doesn't matter to me,' Bonni said. 'Aside from placing fifty on Celia losing her lunch in an alleyway and the quarter slots, I don't plan to gamble much, but a show would be kickass. I vote *Thunder*.'

Her friends all turned and stared at her, completely aghast at her confession.

'Won't gamble much?' their voices chimed in unison.

'We're in Vegas, Bonni! It goes without saying. You *need* to gamble,' Fredi nearly shouted.

Bonni furrowed her brows. 'Why does it go without saying?'

'We're in Vegas,' Ava repeated. 'You gotta gamble.'

Celia waggled her eyebrows, proclaiming loudly, 'Yeah, and what happens in Vegas stays in Vegas.'

Chapter 3

The women hit the casino with an energy that had Bonni bursting with anticipation. She hung behind the others and watched them chatter. Ava and Fredi had their arms linked as they followed Celia, who was leading the way through the crowd like a pro.

Bonni knew just how badly she needed this trip with her besties, and she was determined to have a great time. Nothing was going to ruin it. The last few months, she'd been so deep in a case that coming up for air was near impossible. She'd had no life. Work, home for sleep and fresh clothes, then back to work. Her only release had been working out in the police-station gym. A girl can only do that for so long.

Bonni laughed at tiny Celia easily cutting a swathe through the crowd between the rows and rows of slots packed full with people. Gone was the practical mom who thought only of her kids. In her place, Bonni was beginning to see snippets of the wild child from college emerging. Ava looked over her shoulder and tipped her head in Celia's direction. They winked at each other, knowing what the other was thinking.

Shenanigans were about to begin.

Ava unhooked her arm from Fredi's and dropped back to Bonni. 'It certainly didn't take long for her to get her groove back. We might be in for some drama.' She didn't have to whisper so Celia wouldn't hear as the din of the casino nearly swallowed up her words, enough so that Bonni had to strain to hear.

Bonni giggled, and said, 'I don't even know what to think. But whatever, she's been wound up so tight for far too long, trying to make ends meet. I can't believe Dickhead is fighting her on child support. The man is a cardiac surgeon while she's hustling for freelance jobs that she can fit around the kids' schedules. Men can be such asshats sometimes. She needs to let loose.'

Ava nodded seriously. 'My last project, I was analyzing spreadsheets until I thought my eyes would bleed. And then, of course, not being appreciated. I'm not thrilled with the corporate-world rat race, let me tell you. Getting some rest and relaxation this weekend is just what the doctor ordered for all of us!'

The group followed Celia around until she finally stopped and declared, 'These are the slots we're going to play.'

They stood in front of a bank of video-style games with a multitude of buttons, multiple wheels, flashing lights and all sorts of rumbling and pinging sounds. Bonni had no idea what to make of it.

She looked at them. 'Holy Hannah! What happened to the old-style slots, the one-armed bandits?'

'Oh my God, seriously, Bonni? You're a cop. In the fraud division, no less. You should know all about these!'

'Come on, Celia, I have nothing to do with gaming. In Canada, gaming is legislated at a provincial level, and the Ontario Lottery and Gaming Commission oversees things in Ontario. And I'm local law enforcement, not a fed.' Bonni eyed the machines.

'What's with all those buttons?' She tapped her fingers on one of the reels with an almost lifelike-looking dragon blowing fire. 'Look at all the reels – there's, like, six of them.'

Celia stepped forward and explained. 'These are for extra spins. When you play the max –' she touched the big round button printed with 'MAX', and continued – 'if you get a certain line of icons –' she ran her fingers over the images behind the screen and tapped a dragon – 'you get extra spins, which gives you more opportunity to win. Big wins too.'

Fredi looked at her and planted her hands on her hips, head tilted slightly. 'Since when did you become the casino aficionado?'

Celia shrugged her shoulders. 'Colin asks a million *why?* questions about pretty much everything, so I started listening to this podcast that explains how things work. They did one about Vegas. Plus, Mom goes to casinos and she likes to brag about her winnings. These kind of machines are her favorite. Besides, you never know when a piece of knowledge will come in handy.'

'You are the queen of useless information,' Fredi teased.

'It's not useless. Information is power,' Celia retorted.

Bonni slid on to the chair in front of the machine Celia was touching. 'Okay, ladies, enough of the bickering,' she said.

They replied in unison, 'We are not bickering.'

Ava laughed, and said, 'We should've bet how long it would take for us to revert to our old college ways. Come on, we're here to have fun! Bonni, this trip was your idea. You take the first spin, and then we'll all take a machine.'

Bonni stared at the machine. As part of their package, they'd all received $100 in play money to gamble with. Of course, gone were the old ridged discs of old. Now, it was all ones and zeroes on a flimsy barcoded piece of paper. She'd carefully amassed a baggie of quarters, but she might as well use the credit first.

Bonni opened her purse and pulled the voucher out. 'Seems like as good a time as any to use the freebie money.' She drew in a deep breath. 'Here we go.'

She slid the voucher into the money slot and was startled how fast it was sucked in. Seconds later, her machine was loaded up with a hundred dollars' worth of credit.

'I thought you weren't going to gamble?' Fredi teased.

The girls crowded behind her.

Bonni shrugged and cracked her knuckles. 'When in Rome.' She made a surprised face and looked at her besties behind her. 'That pun was totally not intended. Plus, it's free. Now, why don't the rest of you play, and quit staring at me. You'll bring me bad luck or something.'

'Don't worry, honey, we'll play. But Ava's right. This trip was your brainchild, so it's only right you say hello to Lady Luck first.' Fredi stepped behind Bonni and put her hand on her shoulder. 'Giving you some good luck, positive karma or whatever you want to call it.'

'Hmph. Well, gather round, girls, and let's hope for the best.' Bonni chewed her lower lip and pondered the array of buttons in front of her. Not understanding all the numbers or what they meant, she made an instant decision and slapped the Max play button with her palm.

The chorus of gasps behind her made Bonni realize how much money the Max play used up. She felt nauseous. 'Whelp. Guess it's time to break out the quarters.'

Celia squeezed Bonni's shoulder. 'You are living on the edge, girlfriend.'

Bonni didn't answer and watched the reels spin and spin.

They stopped in a line that Bonni thought looked promising. 'Is that good? Did I win something?'

Celia squealed, 'Look, look! You're getting a free play.' Her friends were totally caught up in the antics of the machine and couldn't contain their elation.

'Shh, guys,' Bonni told them.

A crowd began to gather. Bonni hated being the centre of attention, so she kept her gaze on the dragons, wishing the machine would stop with the clanging bells, strobing lights and rumbling. It was a computer – did the programmers really have to make it vibrate like that? The slot machine continued trying to deafen her and shaking as if it were about to launch into space. Bonni lifted her hands away, surprised how interactive it all was.

Three reels on the left stopped on matching gold dragons. Bonni flicked her gaze up to see what that prize was, and the machine started to growl and rumble louder. The three reels on the right continued to spin, then one came to a stop with a whistling that sounded like a pinwheel firecracker. Another gold dragon. Bonni's heart nearly stopped. The roar in her ears drowned out the screams behind her.

Oh my God.

The middle reel trembled to a stop. Another gold dragon. The noise from the machine increased. Bonni's attention was glued to the images of the dragons, and she whispered to them, 'Come on, baby, come on!'

The last reel stopped on a gold dragon, giving her a line of fire-breathers. Bonni blinked, not fully realizing what it meant. She knew she had won, but the crowd behind her erupted into loud cheers and the screaming of her girls was deafening. Then lights flashed, bells rang, and a huge dragon breathing fire rose from the top of the bank of slot machines. How much had she won?

Bonni bolted from her seat.

Behind her, Celia was wailing like a banshee: 'You won, you won, you won!'

Ava shouted, 'Holy crap! I don't believe it.'

Fredi leaned over her shoulder, the only calm one. 'You won, Bonni! You hit the jackpot!'

'Yeah.' Bonni was stunned. 'But not the jackpot. Not possible.' She looked up at all the flashing lights. 'I never win anything.'

'Well, you have now!' The elation in Fredi's voice infected Bonni. 'I don't know how much, but I think it's going to be big.'

Celia pointed up. 'Shit, look, Bon-Bon! That flashing sign says you've won a hundred grand!'

'You've got to be kidding me. I never win anything,' Bonni repeated.

'This is so exciting! It's like something out of a movie! You won, Bonni,' Ava assured her, enthusiasm bubbling out of her.

Bonni was used to pressure and to making decisions under fire, but this was out of her wheelhouse. You don't get anything for free. Her father had drilled that into her as a kid. You work hard, you do a good job, and get rewarded. So winning money at a casino, especially so much money, by simply pressing a button was making it really difficult for her to keep her composure. A hundred grand was nothing to sneeze at. She drew in a deep breath and made a decision that, if she really had won, she'd share it with her friends. It wouldn't seem right otherwise.

Bonni looked down at the flashing buttons on the machine. Then, on a sudden impulse, she punched the payout button. Nothing happened. She pressed it again. Still nothing.

'It won't work,' Celia said, placing her hand over Bonni's. 'You have to wait for an attendant to come and do whatever they do. Anything over a specific amount needs one. It's too much money.'

'I can't believe this.' Bonni shook her head and found herself in the middle of a group hug with her friends.

'Believe it.' Celia told her. 'You're a winner.'

*

Nobody ever tells you about the drama around winning a jackpot. They'd had to wait until a technician and the casino floor manager showed up to verify the win. Then Bonni was interviewed, asked why she was in Vegas and what she planned to do with the money. Given a huge fake check with her name and the amount on it, to have her picture taken. Bonni chose to remain anonymous and collect her money without a big fuss being made but she did ask for a copy of the photo of her with the check.

Bonni had left Celia and Fredi at the slots and asked Ava to come with her, her being a financial brainiac and all. They followed the floor manager to go and do the paperwork. Good thing she knew her social security number and bank account details by heart. She was provided with a Form W-2G and advised that a percentage of her winnings would be in her bank account within twenty-four hours. Bonni was pretty sure this was so that she would keep gambling. The casino advised Bonni that they had to report any gambling winnings over $1,200 to the IRS. Furthermore, she was asked to choose between a lump sum or monthly payments. A lump sum suited her just fine.

Once the details were completed, a manager from the front desk met them on their way back to the casino, all smiles and charm. The hotel would very much like to upgrade their rooms, as a celebratory gesture. Ava gave a whoop of joy before texting the others to get their asses moving. Bonni thought cynically that it was less of a congratulations and more a thank you for all the good publicity her stroke of luck would bring the brand-new hotel. *No, dammit, accept at face value, Bonni!* The cop in her needed a vacation too.

Celia and Fredi came streaming out of the crowd and they all followed the manager to the bank of elevators. They got off on the top floor and were led to a set of impressive double doors. The manager tapped a room key against the door before handing the rest of the key cards to Bonni.

'The bags you left at the check-in will be brought up shortly. Congratulations, Ms Connolly, and welcome to your suite. If you need anything at all, make sure you ring down to the concierge.'

'Thank you.' Bonni was still trying to grasp everything that had happened.

He stood aside, holding the door as the women entered. Bonni stopped dead. 'Would you look at this place!' She couldn't believe the management had upgraded them to this three-bedroom presidential suite. All because she'd won. 'Wow, so amazing! I'm speechless,' Bonni whispered. 'This is the lap of luxury. Can you believe this?'

'No, I can't! I've only ever seen rooms like this on a movie screen!' Ava squealed.

Bonni watched her girls as they investigated the suite. Celia wandered behind the in-room bar, inspecting the liquor, while Ava took in the view. Fredi came out of the bathroom, impressed with the high thread count of the towels. Since the day they'd met, in a women's studies class in college – their professor had opted to base the seating arrangements on the students' first names, the names their mothers had given them, rather than the patriarchal hand-me-downs of their last names – and bonded when they couldn't stop snickering. They'd always had each other's backs, and she couldn't be more grateful. Bonni wondered if they were still young and silly enough to do the crazy things they'd done in college. Lord, the dancing, the tequila shots, and climbing that damn water tower. Bonni smiled and drew in a big sigh, so unbelievably happy right now.

'Guys, we need to kick the vacation up a notch. We're going shopping, and then we're asking the concierge to point us in the direction of the hottest club in town. My treat.'

Celia poured a shot of tequila and waggled the bottle in Fredi's direction. Fredi rolled her eyes but came over to line up another three glasses. Ava walked over and wrapped an arm around Bonni's waist, saying, 'You don't need to treat us! Our original plan is already awesome! The money you won, that's, like, down-payment-on-a-house kind of money, even after the taxes.'

Fredi snorted. 'That's our Ava. Heart of a dreamer, brain of an accountant.'

'Hey! Just because I believe in happy endings doesn't mean I can't be realistic too!' Ava countered. 'Money can make you or break you.'

Bonni slung her arm around Ava's shoulders and guided her toward the bar. 'You are absolutely correct, but this is free money. I won it on the hotel's dime. I'm not going out and wagering it all on blackjack, just sprinkling a little magic on this girls' weekend. And then I'll sock the rest away for the Virginia move.' She gave Ava a kiss on the cheek. 'Now calm the hell down and enjoy yourself.'

'Yes, ma'am.' Ava took a glass when Celia began passing out the tequila shots.

'Well, I'm certainly not going to argue with you. I haven't been to a club since my ill-fated why-didn't-any-of-you-stop-me? bachelorette party.' Celia held her shot glass up.

Fredi jabbed a finger at Celia accusingly. 'Excuse me, I don't remember every single thing from that night, but I do remember telling you the statistics on divorce and you pooh-poohing me, saying you were in lurrvvve.'

'I was blitzed out of my mind! You should've kidnapped me.'

'But then you wouldn't have your kids,' Ava pointed out.

Celia sighed, swirling the shot gently. 'That's true. Everything that happened, it happened for a reason. My kids.'

'And me winning a hundred grand is for a reason too. C'mon, enough chattering, let's get this party started!' Bonni shouted, raising her tequila glass to her friends.

They clinked their glasses before downing the shots and slamming their glasses on the bar in unison. Bonni felt the burn go down her throat and into her veins. She was determined that this was going to be a once-in-a-lifetime, no-holds-barred trip. Bonni leaned over the bar to grab the bottle of tequila.

'One more round, ladies, before we go hit the shops. After all, someone has to be the winner of the Celia Pukes pool, and I'm feeling lucky!'

'Hmm, taking shots like that, I've got to wonder if you might be the one we should be wagering on!' Fredi warned.

'Nah, are you kidding? You know I don't drink much.' Bonni waved off her friend's remark.

Fredi slapped five dollars down on the bar. 'Who's in?'

Before Bonni knew it, money was on the bar. 'Wow, guys, talk about a no-confidence vote.'

Chapter 4

After an afternoon of shopping (and some napping – stupid jet lag!), Bonni stood under the flattering lights in the envy-inducing bathroom off her private bedroom. The girls insisted she have the master bedroom with the king-sized bed and en suite bathroom, since this was all her doing. They didn't have to pressure her too hard, but it did make her feel a tad uncomfortable.

Showered and standing in her bra and panties, both bought today, Bonni was pleasantly pleased at her reflection. Being on the job meant daily gym visits, tough workouts and a body that was fit and lean. She nodded, glad the hard work had paid off.

But her hair!

'Fuck, what a mess.'

She made a face and scrubbed her fingers through her disheveled locks, newly trimmed just that afternoon to hang just to her shoulders, her bangs skimming her brows. She had product that would at least calm the strands. Digging through her bag, she squirted some cinnamon-scented oil into her palm and rubbed it through the dampness. She left it to dry naturally and shook her head a bit to encourage the straight locks to fluff up.

Bonni rummaged through her little makeup bag, hoping everything was still usable and hadn't dried up. To her satisfaction, she managed to apply eye makeup and not look like a raccoon.

'Not bad,' she told her reflection in the mirror. 'Oh, where did I put that lipstick?' She'd taken the saleswoman's advice and bought a new deep-red lipstick that complemented the dress she had treated herself to.

She leaned toward the mirror and carefully applied the guaranteed-twenty-four-hour color.

Done, she stepped back and scrutinized herself. The slinky little black dress the girls had talked her into looked pretty damn good. She'd spent a small fortune on it and some shoes – another uncharacteristic impulse, but, hey, you only live once, right? And tonight was a celebration. They'd already had a scrumptious late lunch, and now it was time to live it up. She swung her hips and liked how the beaded, flared skirt swung at mid-thigh.

'When you're sexy and you know it,' Bonni crooned softly, then placed her palms on her cheeks when they heated up. She was feeling a little silly and, you know what? She was liking the silly.

She pointed her foot and checked out her shoes. The heels were ridiculously high, but she loved them. They matched the dress perfectly. Being a cop didn't lend itself to many occasions where she could strut her stuff. Maybe she'd have to add a few pairs of heels to the scads of sneakers, boots and work shoes she already owned.

'I can chase down a runner, I'm going to make sure I don't fall off these heels.' Bonni paced a little in the bathroom, her heels making a satisfying clicking sound, and she only wobbled once.

Grabbing the little sparkly clutch (yet another impulse buy), she shoved in a few items she might need and slid the delicate beaded chain over her shoulder. Now to face her biggest critics.

'Time to get this show on the road,' she told her reflection.

Bonni took a deep breath and pulled the door open.

The girls were laughing and carrying on in the other room. There was a pop, followed by more laughter.

'Quickly, pour it, don't spill a drop!' she heard Celia say in the living room.

'What are you guys up to in here?' Bonni asked, as she entered the central living area. She caught her breath at the spectacular sunset she could see through the windows.

'Champagne!' Celia crowed.

'Holy shit. What happened to you?' Fredi blurted out.

'What's the matter?' Bonni asked. 'Is something wrong? You guys said it looked good in the store.' She glanced down at her dress.

'No, no,' Fredi assured her. 'You look fabulous. It's just I've never seen you so wonderfully dressed up before. I think I may have to make you model some of my wedding dresses.'

Bonni tipped her head to the side and stuck a hand on her hip. 'Seriously? Me, a model for wedding dresses? When the possibility of me getting married is as remote as—'

'You winning a hundred grand in Las Vegas?' Ava quipped, and Bonni shot her a look. Ava blew her a kiss.

'I highly doubt there's a wedding in my future. My job isn't the best for raising a family or having a significant other. Plus, I'm far too independent and complicated.'

'True, dat,' Fredi said, and then ducked when Bonni reached out to swat her.

'Never say never,' Ava argued.

'Celia! Back me up here!' Bonni was looking for someone to take her side.

Celia had been uncharacteristically quiet up until now. 'Look,' she said, 'No one's saying you're going to get married tonight—'

'We would never let you have a drunken elopement, like in a romance novel,' Ava stated, shaking her head.

Fredi regarded Ava for a beat before continuing, 'But, come on, Bonni, you don't know what tomorrow will bring.' Bonni was a little shocked by Fredi's uncharacteristic philosophical musing.

'Matrimonial bliss aside,' Celia said with a nod, eyeing Bonni up and down. 'You're definitely gonna get some tonight. Va-va-*vroom*!'

Bonni furrowed her brows. 'Maybe I'd better change then. I want to have a good time with you guys, not spend the whole night fighting off drunken married tourists looking for a vacation fling.'

Ava jumped up and put her arm around her. 'Hey, remember what you said in the store. Turn the cop brain off and stop being so cynical, dammit! You look fantastic. We all do.'

Celia stood up and did a little pirouette in the middle of the living room. 'I do look pretty damn hot. Maybe I'll take a page from Bon-Bon's book and cut loose too, look for a Mr Right Now.'

'Oh Lord, this is the Kappa Sigma Bachelor Auction all over again.' Fredi rolled her eyes.

'It was *not* my fault the twins didn't know how to share,' Celia defended.

Fredi looked at her watch. 'What time is the limo coming? 'Cause speaking of sharing, we should go share our sexiness with the world.'

'Not before we drink some of that champagne,' Bonni said. 'It'll only go flat before we get back and we still have a few minutes. Bottoms up, ladies.'

She poured them each a glass and they clinked them together.

Fredi shivered. 'I've never been able to get used to champagne. But if we're starting off like this, who's got the bail money?'

Everyone looked at Bonni.

She nodded her head. 'Yeah, yeah, yeah, I've got my badge. Don't worry.' She pulled it from her clutch and held it up before tucking it back inside. 'But no gun. I left that locked up at home.'

Celia craned her neck and commented, 'I don't see any cuffs in there.'

Bonni gave her a withering look while Ava and Fredi let out a whoop.

After a few more drinks the girls rode the elevator down and climbed into the waiting limo. They were flying high by the time they arrived at the club. The bouncers checked their names against their lists before letting them through the velvet ropes.

'Wow, VIP service or what?' Ava gushed.

'Oh my God, this place is fantastic,' Celia said, leading the way, her hips swaying to the thumping beat. 'We're gonna have some fuuunn.'

'The concierge assured me this is the It place right now. We might even see a celebrity or two. There should be a table reserved for us in the VIP section, with bottle service.'

Ava was gawking at everything. Bonni took her hand and led her through the crowd. 'Don't trip,' she instructed.

'Stunning,' Ava said. 'The dance floor is so packed!'

Bonni looked around. She felt a little exposed, in this dress, among hordes of people, and without her gun. Of course, if she had it, there'd be nowhere to put it. Bonni rolled her shoulders.

Go with the flow.

'Ladies, your table.' The hostess gestured to a raised seating area. They looked at each other and giggled.

'You first, Bonni. Since this is your winning night.' Fredi stood aside.

Bonni climbed the clear steps, lit with internal mini-lights, to a beautiful spot set up like a private living room with comfortable couches, throw pillows and low tables. Three of the walls were strung with a zillion little beads that shimmered and shifted in the air, reflecting prisms of light. It was totally magical. Like a fairyland. The girls settled in after Fredi had slipped the hostess a tip. The round center table had a bottle of champagne chilling in a bucket.

Bonni said, 'This must be the night of champagne, but I didn't order ahead.'

Ava leaned forward and plucked an envelope from underneath the bucket. 'It's addressed to you, Bonni.' She handed it to her friend.

Celia clapped her hands. 'You have a secret admirer already!'

'I do not!' Bonni pulled the card out of the envelope. '*A little something to help you enjoy your first night in Las Vegas. Gladiators Management.*'

'Wow.' Celia said. 'Money sure begets money.'

'That's unbelievable,' Ava commented.

'Why couldn't they give us a bottle of Jack Daniels?' Fredi pouted.

'I'll get you a bottle of Jack Daniels, or whatever you'd like,' Bonni told her. 'The Southerner in you is showing,' she teased.

'Ain't nothing wrong with Jack!' Fredi defended her favorite alcoholic beverage.

Luckily, a waitress appeared before the conversation could turn heated. Fredi was very protective of her Jack. 'Good evening, ladies. What can I get for you?'

'I think my friend would prefer Jack Daniels instead of the champagne. Ava, Celia, do you want the champagne, or something different?' Bonni wanted to make sure her friends had what they wanted. Nothing but the best for her besties.

'Why don't we keep the champagne for later? I'd like to get a cocktail – is there a house specialty?' Ava inquired.

Celia perused the bottle menu, making little gasping noises at some of the prices. 'Ya know what? I'm going to get a cocktail too.'

After a few more minutes of discussion Bonni opted to help Fredi demolish the Jack and the waitress left to fill their orders. Bonni settled into her comfortable chair. She could definitely get used to this. Her job and her temperament didn't lend themselves to gambling, but the thrill of getting lucky was a seductive one.

'The music's amazing,' she shouted, loving how the throbbing music crept into her blood.

Ava nodded. She was the super-ladylike one. But when music was playing she could be an animal. She jumped up, reaching for Bonni's hand. 'Come on, let's go dance. This is my favorite song.'

Bonni stood. 'Every song is your favorite song, Ava. You should have been a professional dancer, you know that.'

'Things in life take you down different paths to the one you started out on.'

Moments later they were out in the crowd on the dance floor, grooving to the music and having the time of their lives. Bonni let the music, and her mild buzz, smother her feelings of self-consciousness.

Not only did she feel good, she looked good too. Let them look. Now she was glad she'd splurged on her dress and shoes. She ran her hands up her sides, loving the way the dress rode over her flesh, then pushed her fingers into her hair so it swung about her shoulders.

A hit song from a popular movie soundtrack came on and Fredi and Celia joined them on the floor, leaving the VIP security to watch over their stuff. They strutted to the song, doing the risqué moves that were in the music video. Shaking their butts and giving a playful slap at the precise moment. Laughing and having a ball.

Bonni twirled with her hands up over her head, feeling like a sexy and confident woman She was having a fabulous time. So were her friends. What more could she ask for?

Chapter 5

Quinn was doing his usual ritual for the night before a tournament began: sitting at the bar and chilling with a drink. One of the highest-payout poker tournaments started tomorrow. And he planned to win it. His plane had landed a couple of hours ago and he'd headed straight to his favorite club to get himself into the Vegas vibe. He was here to try and woo Lady Luck. Again. She was an elusive bitch and, when she was generous, it was good, but he also knew she could be equally tight-fisted.

Quinn gazed around the room, taking in the crowd. It was going on 11 p.m., and he knew he needed to get some rest, but he had tossed back his Scotch and was now ready for a second. He was far too wound up to settle down just yet.

The dance floor was packed, and no one intrigued him enough to go and cut in. Quinn was one of those rare male specimens who actually liked to dance. His mother had made sure he and his brother knew their way around the dance floor. He hadn't enjoyed it much as a kid, but he'd appreciated it when he discovered girls and learned that women loved a man who could dance. He tapped the bar with his fingers, indicating that he wanted another drink.

They knew him here. The barman placed a glass in front of him.

'Thanks, man.' Quinn wasn't in a talkative mood.

'You in the tournament?' the bartender asked him.

Quinn nodded. 'Yep.'

'I heard it's pretty tough this time.' The bartender was chatty tonight.

Quinn shrugged his shoulders. 'They're all tough.' He sipped his drink and turned back to the crowd.

A familiar song came on. One that women seemed to love and which usually led to a slew of drunk chicks trying to move seductively in sky-high heels. This ought to be interesting.

He sat back and watched the crowd. Then the sea of people parted and he saw her. Quinn froze, the glass to his lips. She was in the perfect position on the dance floor. A spotlight bathed her in its beam, the beads on her dress reflecting the light, shimmering and giving her a soft glow. The thin straps clung to her shoulders and the sheath hugged her lean curves, ending high on her thighs. She had fantastic legs. He put the glass down and swallowed. Her skin was pale and a complete contrast to her dark hair.

Quinn was mesmerized. Lord, he wanted to unwrap and discover everything about her. The sensation of the silky dress beneath his hands, and the heat of her body . . . She was magnificent.

Quinn stood.

It appeared she was with friends. They were an attractive group of women and he was surprised no men had claimed them yet. Of the four of them, though, *she* was the one who had caught his eye. Quinn smiled.

The inherent grace in her dance moves, even as she nearly clocked her blonde friend in the eye with an enthusiastic hand wave, told him all he needed to know. She would be just as sensual underneath him. In his bed. He preferred not to pick up women the night before a tournament, as he didn't want any distractions in the morning, but she intrigued him and he needed to meet her.

After about fifteen minutes the group of women bounced off the dance floor and up to their table. To have a table like that in a club like this meant there was cash flow. He watched as his brunette beauty slipped a twenty to the security guy. If she had money, she wouldn't be after his.

'Those women –' Quinn leaned sideways toward the bar and pointed – 'what are they drinking?'

'I can find out for you, Mr Bryant.'

Quinn sat back on his stool and kept his eye on the women. He didn't want to lose track of them if they began to get ready to leave before he could play his hand.

'Mr Bryant, they're drinking house specialties and they ordered a bottle of Jack Daniels.'

'Okay, send them over a round of the cocktails.'

'Yes, sir.'

Nursing his second drink, Quinn saw the waitress take the tray of drinks. Leaving his glass and a sizeable tip on the bar, he moved to their table, but hung back until they were served. The waitress spoke and the woman he was interested in glanced around. He caught his breath when they made eye contact. Her eye color was hard to determine in the shifting light from the dance floor. But her eyes were expressive, almost a smoky grey, and he was snagged by them in a way he hadn't thought possible. It was the first time he'd ever been rattled under the intense scrutiny of a woman and he was shocked when his heart actually did a double beat. It was like she saw right through him, past his outer shell and deep down through the layers. But that was impossible. He never showed anything. A professional poker player needed the proverbial poker face, and he could keep emotion off his features with the best of them. She smiled and nodded. He returned the gesture. The other women all turned around to look, but he saw only her.

Time to ante up.

Fredi said, 'Looks like Bonni really does have a secret admirer.'

'Oh my God. Bonni! I told you!' Ava whispered.

'Uhm, is it me, or did the sexual tension up in here suddenly get *thick*?' Celia declared.

'We're all going to need oxygen soon,' Fredi replied. 'Come on, Bonni, invite him up.'

Bonni barely heard her friends talking. She was pinned to the spot by this man's stare. No one had ever looked at her like that before and it was paralyzing, in a wonderfully erotic way. Her breaths came more shallowly. Her heart raced, pumping her blood heavy and hot through her veins. This man gave her all the sensual feels. She forced herself to breathe, but she still couldn't move a muscle.

Bonni willed her body to behave and lifted her drink, sipping and keeping her gaze glued to his over the rim of the glass. It gave her a few moments to gather her thoughts, make a quick plan and decide to do a little harmless flirting. Flirting never hurt anybody, right? This sort of thing happened all the time in Vegas. Probably nothing would come of it.

He walked to the stairs, and Bonni watched him. He moved fluidly, with a leashed power that she could almost feel. Suddenly nervous, Bonni gulped the rest of her drink.

'Bonni!' Celia was nearly bouncing on her toes as she blurted out, 'He's coming. He's coming.'

'I see that, don't need a play-by-play. Be quiet. I'm nervous enough.' Bonni swallowed and did her best to keep her composure, placing the glass on a low table. She wanted her hands free. Why? She wasn't entirely sure yet.

'Ladies, good evening.' He smiled, and Bonni could have sworn she heard a collective sigh from her friends. He had a fantastic smile that reached his deep blue eyes and she was drawn into the depths of them. Oh, and his voice was intoxicating, making her feel drunk. Or maybe that was the champagne, mixed with the other drinks they'd had?

No, it was him. Not the drinks.

She gave herself a mental shake, recognizing that the evening had taken a very intriguing shift, and stepped forward. 'Please, come join us. Thank you so much for sending the round over.' Her voice quivered a little bit and she pressed her tongue to the back of her teeth, desperately trying to get herself back under control.

'It was my pleasure.' He homed right in on Bonni. 'I couldn't help but notice you on the dance floor. I've been watching you for a little while.' He didn't mince his words.

'You have? Not sure whether that's creepy or I should be flattered,' Bonni replied, eyeing him a little more thoroughly. Her cop side knew which way it was leaning, but the woman was willing to give this handsome stranger the benefit of the doubt.

He laughed, tipping his head back to expose his tanned and muscular neck. *Oh Lord.* Bonni found herself noticing all the little things about him. How his dark hair brushed the collar of his shirt, the way his shoulders and his powerful arms stretched the fabric that was tucked neatly into a pair of snug jeans that fit perfectly on his slim hips. She had the urge to run her fingers over his muscles and touch him. His looks were a deadly combination and exactly fitted her idea of a dream man. Dark hair, blue eyes, powerful body, tall. She fisted her hands and discovered she was smiling back at him.

'Well, I certainly didn't mean to be creepy. All of you ladies look like you're having a great time and –' he looked directly at Bonni – 'you definitely caught my eye. I couldn't resist sending some drinks over.'

Bonni felt a tremble ripple through her and struggled for something to say that wouldn't reveal how suddenly he was affecting her.

'You don't waste any time, do you?' Bonni was trapped by the intensity of his stare.

'Not when I see something I want. Do you mind if I join you, or do you have other plans?' He took a fraction of a step closer. Bonni felt like she'd been hit by a tidal wave.

Ava scooted to Bonni's side. 'No, no plans. We're just here –' she raised her hand to indicate the club – 'dancing, having a few drinks. Some fun. It's our first night.'

'Ah. I just got in myself.' He smiled at Celia.

'Alone?' Bonni asked, then bit her tongue. Now she was the one being borderline creepy. But she had to know if he was with anyone. If he was, then the brakes would come on with a screeching halt.

'Yes.' He smiled. 'Alone.' He lowered his voice and pinned her with a look. 'For now, anyway.'

Oh my. Bonni drew in a breath and didn't reply. Ninety per cent of her coworkers were men, but there, she was just one of the guys. With this hot, polite, single, seemingly sober man pursuing her, she didn't know what to do. Luckily, her friends didn't seem to have any such issues.

'Please excuse my friend. She's severely jet lagged, since it's, like, 2 a.m. for her back home, and it's clearly affecting her manners. I'm Celia, that's Ava and Fredi, and this, this is Bonni. She's alone too. Except for us, of course.'

Bonni was a little surprised that Celia didn't start extolling her virtues and giving him her entire life story.

'I'm Quinn – Quinn Bryant – and it's a pleasure to meet you all.'

Bonni watched him interact with her friends. She sensed an underlying power in him that she found devastatingly attractive. She was drawn to strong men. Bonni had dated a pushover once and, when the novelty of always getting her way had worn off, she vowed only to date men who could match her in strength. She could already tell that Mr Quinn Bryant fitted the bill.

There is something about this man that has me all flustered in a wonderful way.

'Bonni.' He smiled. Oh, she could have melted into him. The tremor deep in her body was getting harder to contain. He was doing things to her she'd never experienced before, and they'd barely talked and certainly hadn't even touched yet.

She knew, then, that she was destined for delicious disaster.

Chapter 6

Quinn's confidence radiated from him in waves and Bonni broke their eye contact so she could catch her breath. She found herself looking at Ava, who was making big eyes at her, clearly excited that Bonni had the chance to be swept off her feet. Celia and Fredi weren't any help either; they were making silent gestures indicating that they thought Quinn was super-hot. Her mouth dried out and she licked her lips. Quinn had her off balance, and that was a hard thing for someone to do to her. Her dad had always said, if you expect everything, then nothing will be unexpected.

Quinn was definitely unexpected.

Even being so discombobulated by him, she couldn't deny the attraction or how badly she wanted to act on it. Bonni had never been the subject of such heated scrutiny before and she felt almost like a suspect on the other side of an interrogation table. Thinking this, her cop side tried briefly to resurface, but Bonni ruthlessly shoved it down. Not here. Not now.

She was on vacation, thousands of miles away from her job,

and her friends knew to keep her career quiet and references to her social activities off social media. They had her back and they'd take her secrets to the grave.

What happened in Vegas would stay in Vegas, so she was determined to enjoy every moment – starting with Quinn.

He held his hand out for her. 'Let's dance.' It wasn't a question, it was a demand. Bonni's heart did a delightful little flip, although she felt a little resistance to being told what to do. Unless it was from a commanding officer, she didn't take orders. She looked at his hand. It was big and rugged but there were no callouses. Oh, what he might be able to do with those hands. She shook herself. *Stop getting ahead of yourself. He could still turn out to be an asshat.* But the draw between them was too powerful to resist.

Bonni looked up at him and reached out. The second their fingertips touched, she drew in a sharp breath, fairly certain electricity was arcing between them. A slow, sensual smile curved on his lips as his fingers tightened on hers. Had he felt it too?

Then and there, Bonni decided. She wanted . . . no . . . *had* to be with this man. They'd start on the dance floor, but her intuition told her the night would end with them in bed together. She darted a glance at her friends again. This was supposed to be a girls' trip, but she was about to go off with a man, something she'd never done before, so spontaneously.

Relief flooded through Bonni at their bright smiles.

'Let's go. Your friends don't look like they're opposed to me sweeping you away for a little while.' Quinn gave her hand a gentle tug, his fingers caressing her palm.

'Sweep away,' she told him, and followed him down the steps. As they stepped on to the dance floor, the fast-paced music switched into a sexy, slow tune.

'Perfect timing,' he said in a low and husky voice as he reached for her.

Goosebumps rose when his hands rested at her waist. Oh, wow, it had been way too long since she'd been held or even touched by a man. So long she'd forgotten what it felt like. She liked how Quinn was reminding her.

Bonni moved deeper into his embrace, his arms slipping around her, their clothes the only barrier between them. She sighed and reached up, sliding her hand across his shoulders leisurely until her fingers touched the warmth of the back of his neck, loving the feel of his steely muscles.

She closed her eyes and rested her cheek on his shoulder. What an apropos song to be playing – 'The First Time Ever I Saw Your Face' sung by Roberta Flack. Such wonderful words, which made Bonni's heart swell as they swayed together, quietly, seductively. Their bodies spoke louder than words ever could.

Quinn pulled her even closer until she was flush against him, hip to shoulder and his knee edged gently between her thighs. He had great instincts and knew exactly what she needed, and this was it. His heart pounded next to hers. Bonni forgot where she was and felt the last of her real-world stress melt away as she floated into a world of pure sensation. The sound of the music. The brush of his body against hers. The scent of him. The look in his eyes.

All she needed to know was what he tasted like.

The song ended and Bonni didn't move from his embrace. She waited, not wanting to break the magical moment between them. He eased his grip on her, and she looked up at him. They stared at each other and she took in everything. She never wanted to forget this moment.

'Thank you.' He spoke softly, so only she could hear.

'Thank *you*,' Bonni echoed.

Even as a child, Bonni had been able to read people, through body language and the microexpressions on a face. She knew the signals a person's eyes gave. She could tell if someone was lying, or telling the truth, or trying to recall a memory. Quinn's eyes were clear, steady, and she saw an honesty in the deep blue that eased her naturally suspicious nature. Going off with a complete stranger was not her style, but there was something about him that reassured her. She couldn't quite put her finger on it, but she felt safe and that he was trustworthy. Hopefully, her instincts were right. But she was in Vegas for just a few days, and only romantics built castles in the air after a single dance.

Bonni still didn't step away from Quinn, waiting for him to make the next move. Part of her wanted the delicious anticipation to continue, to enjoy the slow build toward the inevitable explosion. And part of her was starving and ready to skip the appetizers and get to the main event. She held her breath, waiting.

'Looks like it's another slow song.' Quinn tightened his grip again and led her into a tender swaying.

'So it does.' Bonni whispered her reply.

'I like how you feel in my arms.' His mouth was close to her ear, and she stepped into him.

'I like how I feel in your arms.' The intimacy in his deep voice had her all aflutter. Bonni wanted to turn her face toward him, but instead she breathed into his neck. His scent filled her, and she wanted him to fill her in other ways too. Being wrapped up by him, surrounded by him, the way he held and touched her, it woke up her sexual nature. Something she'd buried so deep for so long. She'd dated, of course, guys like Greg, who were easy to walk away from. It was better to focus on her work and ignore her sexual needs. Getting tangled up in relationships just led to getting hurt. But, now, here with Quinn, she was beginning to realize how wonderful it could be with the *right* man.

His hand slid down her back, leaving a fiery trail, and Bonni pressed herself into him. She wanted more, and he delivered. He used his grip on her hips to turn her so that her back was to his chest. She could feel his taut body, the heat radiating through his clothes and caressing the bare skin of her back. His arm rested across her stomach, holding her against him, his hand tantalizingly close to her breasts.

'I'm glad I saw you on the dance floor.' He spoke and pressed his lips to the curve of her neck, his breath sensitizing her skin. Bonni shivered, her ass pressing against his groin, and Quinn groaned, which made her body flush with erotic heat.

Oh Lord. He's pushing all my buttons.

'Me too.' Was that her voice? It was throaty with arousal.

They swayed like that for long moments before he spun her again. She looked up into his eyes, his pupils dilated so wide the black nearly eclipsed the blue of his irises. She kept her arms tight around his shoulders, letting him lead, clinging to him and following his body around the dance floor. She didn't have to do a thing, except hold him. He swayed them to the music, carrying them through the tune as if they were the only couple dancing. Bonni had never been so immersed in a dance or in music before. The lights were low, the pace had slowed and they melded together. Bonni smiled to herself when his erection rose. 'I want you to come with me to my room tonight,' he told her.

'Yes.' How could she answer any other way?

He regarded her, a smile curving his very kissable mouth. In the rare event that Bonni was involved with a man, she usually kept him at arm's length. As she had told her friends, her job pretty much doomed any relationship, so she never got emotionally invested and was always prepared to walk away. Better to leave them than for them to leave her. But this man – oh, this man – had turned her world topsy-turvy in two songs.

'So then. Shall we?' He leaned down and brushed his lips across her hair.

She nodded, and couldn't find her voice right away. Bonni pointed to her friends. 'I need to check in with my friends and get my bag.'

'Lead the way.' Quinn kept his hand at the small of her back as they headed to the VIP section.

Before they went up the stairs she turned and held up a hand. 'Would you mind waiting here for a moment?'

'Of course. Just don't forget about me.' He cupped her face and brushed a thumb across her lips. She gasped a little at the sensation, her lips parting. Quinn was starting to bend down when a flash of light distracted them both. Bonni turned to look, flushing when she saw Ava practically hanging over the railing with her cell phone.

'I'll, um, I'll be right back.' She made a beeline for her friends, hearing Quinn chuckle behind her.

When she reached their table Celia and Fredi started applauding, while Ava shoved her phone in Bonni's direction. 'Look at how cute you guys are together! You fit together perfectly!'

Fredi elbowed her way forward to see. 'God, Ava, you totally cock-blocked her. He was going to kiss the hell out of her.'

Ava spun on a heel, her auburn waves swinging and catching the light like sparks of gold, to face Fredi, wobbling a little. 'I did not! He's right there waiting for her! She's totally going to get his cock!' She tucked a wayward strand behind an ear.

Bonni felt her cheeks heat up again and swore she heard Quinn laugh, despite the now thumping music. 'Okay, you guys have clearly had a lot to drink. Maybe I shouldn't go.'

'Oh, screw that,' Celia said. 'We're big girls and we can take care of ourselves.'

'When's the last time you've been out on the town like this? I'm the one who is always aware of her surroundings, unlike you guys.' She looked at them as sternly as she could. 'Remember that night when you were only wearing mini-skirts and halter tops and snuck into the—'

Celia held up her hand. 'Nope, you're not going to bring that up. I refuse to let you. Besides, the lock was broken on the gate. Anyone would have tried climbing up the water tower.'

'No, they wouldn't have, not in December!' Bonni was still aghast at the whole debacle.

Fredi slapped Bonni's clutch against her chest and she fumbled to take it. 'Yes, and I seem to remember that one time when you got plastered and stole a candy bar from that 7-Eleven and then felt so guilty you went back in and gave the guy twenty bucks for it. It was college, and you weren't even a cop yet! Get over it.'

Away from Quinn's magnetism, Bonni began to second-guess herself. Biting her lip, she tapped her clutch against her thigh. Knowing the signs, Ava caught her gaze. Bonni had always thought she had beautiful eyes, golden with flecks of blue, and right now they expressed myriad emotions. Ava was giving her orders: 'Oh, no, you don't. You are not bailing on that man. Celia put condoms in your bag and Fredi turned on the Find Your Friend app on your phone.'

'My phone? How did you get in my phone?'

Fredi shot her a look that plainly said, *Don't ask stupid questions.*

Celia put down her third cocktail with a snap and stood up to shake Bonni's shoulders. 'Look, Bon-Bon, you haven't been laid since that limp pancake Greg. It's time to clear out the cobwebs from your hoo-haa, you know, and get your vacation fling on.'

Bonni glanced back at Quinn and saw him chatting with one of the security guards. Good God, she hoped he hadn't heard Celia's remark . . .but he was looking like he had all the time in the world to wait for her. A gold star for him.

'Okay, the club has my card on file so that'll take care of the tab. I'll text you when I know where we're going. Does someone have money for a cab? Do you all have your room keys?'

Bonni thought these were perfectly reasonable questions, but Fredi rolled her eyes. She nudged Celia out of the way and forced Bonni to turn around, before pushing her toward the stairs. 'Hey, Quinn!' Fredi shouted. 'Where are you staying?'

Quinn broke off his conversation and raised an eyebrow as Fredi practically shoved Bonni down the stairs. 'I'm at the Gladiators.'

'What a coincidence! So are we. Bonni won't have far to go in the morning then. Bye now!'

Fredi gave a little mocking wave before strutting back to the table. Bonni wasn't sure whether to be grateful or horrified. Quinn reached out to take her free hand and she looked at him. 'Still in?' he asked.

Oh, those eyes.

Bonni knew there was really only one response you can make when you're about to start a Vegas vacation fling.

'I'm all in.'

Chapter 7

Bonni waited while Quinn exited the taxi and reached back in for her. She placed her hand in his and he helped her out of the car, making sure she was steady on her unfamiliar high heels before closing the door. He was every inch the gentleman, but there was an undercurrent that spoke to her long-dormant wild side.

They walked through the lobby to a bank of elevators, the only sounds the noises from the casino and the clicking of her heels. His hand was on the small of her back again, her body fitting into the curve of his arm. Once inside an elevator, he pulled her fully into his embrace. She let her head fall back and he lowered his until their lips almost touched.

'You were quiet on the drive.' His breath whispered over her cheek, stoking the fire of her desire.

'It was a short drive.' Bonni turned her head slightly, exposing her neck to him. He knew what she wanted and trembled when he delicately placed a kiss next to her jawline.

'Your neck begs for kisses.' His lips moved against her flesh.

'Ooh.' She sagged into his arms, and he held her tight.

'You're okay with heading to my room? I expect you're all rooming together?' His voice was soft, and questioning.

'As a matter of fact, we are. Yes, I am very okay with visiting your room.' Bonni sighed and draped her arms around his shoulders.

She hoped no one else would get in the elevator with them.

Quinn backed her against the wall, the muscles of his thighs pressing hers, taking teasing nips along her neck. 'I do have a good view of the Strip.'

Feeling adventurous, Bonni slid a hand down to his ass and squeezed. 'It's not the Strip I'm looking to view.'

He chuckled and continued his quest along her neck. 'So long as I'm not the only one stripping.'

Bonni's mind was beginning to fog with passion. 'If you think you'll enjoy the view.'

'Oh, I can promise you I will.' His mouth trailed back up to her cheek and kissed his way to her lips.

'Y-yes, I believe you will. What happens in Vegas stays in Vegas?' she asked him, surprised by the sultry tone in her voice. She wasn't quite sure if she only wanted one night or, perhaps, maybe . . . longer.

'Anything you wish.' He gripped her wrist and Bonni sucked in a quick breath at the sensations fanning out from his touch. With him curved over her, even with her heels putting her at nearly six feet, he was much taller than she was. She felt delicate, feminine and sexy.

'You're trembling,' he said, next to her ear.

'I know,' Bonni whispered.

'I like that.' The tone of his voice, seductive and deep, totally melted her inside and the throbbing between her thighs escalated to wonderfully dangerous levels.

'Ohh.' She was done. His words and touch were seducing her into a puddle, and she was loving every second of it.

She quivered, unable to control herself, and held on to him, which really wasn't necessary, because he had her well in hand, one cradling the back of her head and the other her ass. She knew with every ounce of her being that, if she collapsed, he wouldn't let her fall.

The *ding* of the elevator broke through her haze and Bonni inhaled, taking in his scent before reluctantly stepping from his arms. He kept his hand at the base of her neck, his fingertips pressing in rather possessively, and she liked it.

'Come closer,' he whispered, and pulled her to his side, sliding his arm around her shoulder.

The elevator door opened and a bunch of loud kids in bathing suits and carrying towels exploded into the elevator.

'Going down?' the oldest-looking one asked.

'Nope,' Quinn said. 'Up. You're going for a ride first.'

'Aww,' one of them complained. 'I told you guys it wasn't going down.'

'They're fast elevators; you'll be there in no time,' Quinn told the kids, and struck up a little conversation. He was at ease with them and Bonni liked to see this unexpected side of him.

He glanced at her and smiled, giving her a slow wink that made her belly tumble a bit. She leaned into him and watched the kids. They didn't seem to care that she and Quinn were in the elevator, and did some shoving and pushing, as boys do.

The car stopped and he dropped his hand to rest at the curve of her waist, guiding her out. Her body seemed to have a mind of its own and heat rushed down to settle with a fire in her belly.

She heard him chuckle as he followed her.

'Have fun, boys,' he said to the kids, and then they were in the silence of the corridor. He took her hand. 'I'm down there.'

'Lead the way.' Bonni liked how he was taking control. For once, she could relax. Give up the need to be in charge. The need to steer events. The need to be in control.

She was still feeling the sensuality of his touch, glad the interruption of the kids hadn't interrupted their growing connection.

'Here we go.' He pulled out the key card and wasted no time whisking her into his room. She had barely crossed the threshold before he swept her up into his arms.

Bonni was surprised. 'You can't carry me.'

'Of course I can.' He dipped his head and found her lips. Bonni placed her palm on his cheek, rough with a light stubble. She held his face, once again welcoming the responsiveness of her body to his simple kiss.

'This is where I've wanted you since we met.' He stood back after laying her on the bed. 'I want to look at you.' Bonni was unable to be motionless. She felt as if her clothes had fallen away and he was able to see beneath her dress. It ramped up her arousal to fever pitch.

'Lie still,' he instructed.

It was one of the hardest things she'd ever had to do. She breathed in shallow bursts and wondered if her heart could bear its rapid beating.

'If you keep looking at me like that, there's no way I can be still.' She sat up and reached for him.

'Your beauty astounds me.' Quinn leaned over and ran his hand over the silky fabric of her dress on her thigh. She wriggled again. 'Shh, stop moving.'

'I can't,' she said, with a shaky breath.

'Yes, you can.' He smiled and looked at her from under his

dark brows. Good Lord, this man had her all discombobulated. But in a wonderful way.

He wrapped his fingers around her ankle and she held her breath, finally able to do as he wanted. She froze when his hand traced lightly up to her calf, then back down to touch the strap on her shoe.

'I like these shoes. Maybe we can keep them on.'

She nodded. Her eyes were glued to his as he placed a knee between her legs and his hands at either side of her hips. The bed sank under his weight and she slid closer to him.

Quinn moved down her body and kissed her belly through the fabric of her dress. Heat from his mouth seared her and she flung her arms wide, clutching at the duvet. Quinn then worked his way up, keeping to the middle of her body, and when he was in the valley between her breasts, Bonni arched her back.

'Easy . . . we have all night,' he murmured against her flesh, just above the neckline of the dress.

'You're k-killing me,' she moaned.

'Good.' His voice was muffled against her body.

Quinn wanted to drive her higher. He knew she was turned on, and the rocking of her hips when he pushed a knee between her legs was the reward he was waiting for. More than anything, he wanted her naked and to sink himself into her heat.

But first, he wanted to discover her. Find out what made her tick. What she desired, and how he could pleasure her.

Yet the heat of her against his thigh was difficult to ignore. He inhaled and caught her scent, which was more intoxicating than any alcohol. Cinnamon, soap, citrus and her growing arousal combined in a lethal mixture that he would not soon forget. He rocked into her, and she tightened her thighs on his leg, holding him in place.

Bonni sighed into him. Quinn groaned, unsure how much

longer he'd be able to contain himself. He had to break the kiss, slow things down a bit but still keep her on a knife edge of desire.

She was responsive, and he wasn't surprised. He had sensed her underlying passion when he'd watched her move on the dance floor earlier. Now he was eager for her to move beneath him. She trembled and gasped when he ran his fingertips down her neck, pausing briefly at a throbbing vein, then over her shoulders and down her sides and back up. Quinn's fingertips told him everything he needed to know.

'How about we get this dress off you?' He waited for her reply.

She nodded and began to lift herself up. He was captivated by the rise and fall of her chest, and the way her nipples pushed against the fabric.

The sight of them made him impulsive and he leaned down, gently nibbling on the hardened point through the material.

'Quinn.' Bonni moaned his name, and he looked at her. She nodded, giving him the go-ahead, arousal in her eyes.

Quinn smiled and tugged the dress, slowly dragging it over her breasts, the thrill of anticipation made her nipples harder. She was wearing a lacy bra, one that allowed a seductive glance of her dusky nipples. He couldn't help his growl of delight.

He leaned down again and sealed his lips around the peak of her breast. She gasped and grabbed his head, sliding her fingers into his hair and holding him to her, making little mewling sounds. It was close to making him crazy with desire, and he enjoyed having this power over her.

Lifting his head, he balanced on an elbow and tugged her dress down a little with his free hand. 'Still in?'

'All in,' she replied, and her heavy-lidded gaze ignited him.

Quinn shifted and rose to his knees. 'Then why is this dress still not off?' He pulled it lower.

'Take it off.' Bonni's voice was husky and full of promise.

He slid his hand under her bottom, raising her easily and drew the dress down her legs, moving to stand at the foot of the bed. He gazed at her in wonder.

'That lingerie is incredible.' His words were strained, his jeans not yielding to his erection. Quinn hadn't been expecting the sight that greeted him. Never had he seen a woman who had such lean muscle and such soft curves, with skin that appeared as soft as satin. He could tell her generous breasts were firm, as was her torso, and his gaze traveled past her cute belly button to the soft rise of her beneath her panties. He ached to have those shapely thighs and calves wrapped around his hips, and would welcome the dig of her killer heels in his ass any day. He shook his head. 'You are perfection.'

Bonni laughed, low and seductive. It seemed to grab hold of him by the balls.

She swung her legs over the side of the bed. 'Now, it's my turn.'

She prowled toward him, and it was the sexiest sight he'd ever seen.

'Time to get you naked,' she told him.

He reached for the buttons on his shirt and she pushed his hand away, shaking her head. 'No. I want to.'

He saw the concentration etched on her face as she quickly undid the buttons. Bonni slipped her fingers between the opening of his shirt, and he jumped when she touched his chest as lightly as a butterfly's wing. It rocked him to his core.

'Mmm. Chest hair. I do love a man with chest hair.' She smiled up at him, and he thought he was a goner. 'A little bit of grizzly in a man can be exciting.'

'Have you ever been eaten by a bear?' His voice was a low rumble.

She laughed, tilting her head back, and the graceful elegance of her neck called to him.

'As a matter of fact, I haven't. Why, are you a bear?'

'You did say you liked grizzlies, and Bear was a nickname through college.'

'Well, isn't that a coincidence.' She leaned into him and placed her palms on his chest, brushed them across his hardened nipples. It was his turn to suck in a quick breath.

'Woman, now it's you who's killing me,' he growled.

Bonni liked the responses she was getting from Quinn. They spurred her on. She swept her hands up his chest to his shoulders and pushed the shirt off, drawing it down his arms before tossing it aside. He was glorious to look at. She flattened her palms over his tanned flesh, and the smattering of hair across his muscled chest tickled her palms. Bonni felt lower, over the firm and ridged belly, down until she could dip her fingers inside the waistband of his jeans.

He stiffened, and she stilled, looking up at him. 'Now what do you have planned?' he asked, and the tightness in his voice told her all she needed to know.

'Well, maybe I'll just copy what you did to me. Like, run my fingers around the waist of your jeans until I find the belt buckle.' She touched him and liked the tremor that rumbled through him. 'Then undo said buckle.' The jingle of the metallic catch was loud in the room as she opened it. 'Perhaps, unzip the fly.' She pulled it down slowly. 'Oh, what do we have here?' She reached inside and swept her fingers over his erection.

'You'll find out soon enough.' He lightly placed his hands on her shoulders, as if to steady himself.

Bonni made a point of brushing her hands over him and

smiled when he groaned. She gave a shove and his pants fell around his ankles. Clad only in tight athletic boxers, his bulge was delightfully large, and the silkiness of the shorts enhanced the steely feel of him beneath her fingers. Moving lower, she gently massaged his balls and ran her fingernails along the ridge of his cock.

'And here we are.' Bonni looked into his eyes.

'Yes, here we are,' he said, and slid his hands down her back to the clasp on her bra. He unclipped it and let it fall to the floor. Bonni drew in a soft breath at the shock of the air-conditioned air on her exposed nipples.

'Just as I thought,' he said. 'Gorgeous.'

Before she realized what he was doing, Quinn leaned down and his lips scorched a hot trail over the rise of her breasts. She tangled her fingers into his hair as he pushed her back until the edge of the bed stopped her. She sank down, and fell sideways across the soft duvet.

Without missing a beat, Quinn shucked off his briefs and Bonni was spellbound at the sight of him. She hooked her thumbs around the waistband of her panties.

'Off.' The need for more words was unnecessary.

Quinn came to her, the evidence of his arousal impressive and demanding. 'Your wish is my command, madam.'

He pushed her hands aside and drew her panties lower, letting his hand trail over her skin. The silky garment seemed so fragile in his strong fingers.

He kneeled on the bed between her ankles, forcing her legs wider, leaving her completely exposed, and to a man she'd met only a couple of hours ago. And she wasn't feeling the least bit shy.

'Stunning,' he murmured. 'I've never seen a sweeter pussy.' He placed his hands on her knees, pushing them further apart.

She held her breath when he leaned down and kissed the crease of her thigh.

'Condoms . . . in my purse.'

'Patience, my lovely. We have all night.'

His mouth had a magical touch. She moaned, raising her hips to him, and he slid his hands under her, lifting her even higher to give him better access. His tongue swept along her sensitive folds until he found her clitoris.

'Quinn . . .' His name came out in a hoarse whisper, and she couldn't control the bucking of her hips as he gave her sublime attention. Bonni held his head, not wanting to let him go. Every little thing he did left her wanting more.

His thumb circled her opening, as he found her clit again. His hand and mouth moved in unison, as if their whole purpose in this world was to give her pleasure. Bonni couldn't do anything except lay there and *feel* as she rocketed toward an orgasm.

He was talented, there was no doubt about that, and she didn't even want to think where he'd gained such skills, only that she was the recipient of them now.

'Q–quinn . . . mmm.' Bonni drew in ragged breaths. He held her bottom in a vice-like grip, keeping her up, relentlessly drawing out more and more sensations. She held her breath, clasping at the sheets with her hands. As the wave of pleasure reached its peak, she came apart under him. Unable to keep her body still, she shuddered, and he held her tight, drawing out her release with excruciating delight. She'd been holding her breath, and it whooshed out of her. Gradually, she started to relax, but he wouldn't let her and found another orgasm lurking deep inside her.

'Ahhh.' Bonni's body tensed and she crumpled to the bed in a mind-numbing rush of release that she let take her over the edge into a vast abyss. She closed her eyes and then opened them again to see him looking at her from between her knees.

'My God.' Bonni just lay there, unable to move as he came up to lie beside her. He gathered her, rolling her into him, and she rested her head on his chest.

'That's never . . .' She couldn't find the right words.

'Then I'm glad I was the first.' He pressed a kiss to her temple and ran his hand over her body, comforting and calming, yet keeping the embers of her arousal smoldering.

His erection, insistent and tempting between them, lured her. Bonni reached down and held him, gently squeezing and running her fingers along his length. She sighed, loving the feel of him.

He groaned, and his muscles constricted.

'My purse,' she murmured into his shoulder. He reached over and got it from the table. Bonni let him go and fumbled to open it. The condoms the girls had given her scattered over the rumpled bedsheets.

Quinn chuckled and raised his eyebrows.

'In for a session, are we?' He grinned and poked the packages on the bed.

Bonni felt surprisingly at ease with him. 'A girl has to be prepared.' He chuckled, and she loved the intimacy of the moment. The afterglow of her orgasm lingered, and being snuggled next to him seemed absolutely perfect. 'Well, if truth be told, my friends snuck them into my bag while we were dancing. They are clearly much more prepared than I.'

'I see.' He squeezed his arm on her shoulder. 'Not something that you do on a regular basis?'

'Ha! Far from it. In fact, it's been quite a while since I've slept with anyone,' Bonni found herself admitting. 'How about you?' she asked him quietly, not really sure she wanted to know the answer. Before he could respond, she placed her hand on his chest. 'No, please don't answer that. I don't think I want to know.'

Their gazes met, and Bonni was the first to look away, resting her head back on his shoulder and feeling the rise of his chest when he drew in a big breath. It was the first slightly awkward moment between them.

'Whenever you want to know, just ask,' he told her, which quite nicely moved them past the moment.

Bonni didn't respond, and instead ran her hand across his belly and a bit lower, until her fingers brushed his pubic hair. There was something about this man that made her comfortable. It could be any one of the numerous qualities she was discovering about him: his quiet confidence, his larger-than-life presence, his skill in the sexual department or his ability to sense her mood.

Her passion for him grew again and, before she started thinking too much, Bonni held his dick, enjoying the feel of his steely length in her hand.

She rose up on her elbow and looked into his face. So far, this evening had been full of surprises. Nice surprises. Surprises she hadn't expected in a million years. Quinn's gaze was magnetizing. Bonni looked into his eyes and squeezed his cock. He sucked in a breath but didn't look away from her.

'I think it's time we took advantage of the generosity of my friends.' Bonni held up a condom. 'Don't you?'

Chapter 8

After their first round of passionate sex, they dozed a bit, sleeping in each other's arms before waking up absolutely starving around 3 a.m. Bonni squealed when Quinn snapped open a large towel and spread it on the sheets in front of her. He then dumped all the snacks he'd gone down the hall to get out of a vending machine on it. He put his hands on his hips and stood there, surveying his haul like a mighty hunter-gatherer and staring down at her with amusement in his eyes. Bonni couldn't get enough of looking at him. His magnificent body, sculpted, firm and powerful, and that delicious bulge she ached to get her hands on again, teasing her from behind the shorts he'd dragged on before leaving the room. She could look at him all day.

Sitting under the rumpled sheets, so very naked but not the least bit self-conscious, Bonni began to sort through the goodies he'd brought back.

'You are a complex woman,' Quinn said, as he climbed back in to the bed after shucking off his shorts.

Momentarily distracted by his nudity, it took a beat before Bonni replied, 'How so?'

He pointed to the stash in front of them. 'This. I can't believe, when you're offered anything you'd like from room service, you choose to indulge in mass-produced junk food from a machine.'

Bonni laughed. 'Because it's yummy! I don't even know if room service would deliver this late at night. And I don't know how you do this!' She waved her hands in a huge gesture that encompassed the snacks and the bed.

'What, having breakfast in bed? It's one of my favorite things to do.' He glanced sideways at her and winked. 'Especially when there is a beautiful naked woman beside me.'

She gave him a playful punch on the arm. 'So this isn't the first time you've done it then. You make a habit of having a beautiful woman in your bed for breakfast?' But despite her teasing tone, Bonni found she did not like that possibility in the least. It unsettled her, and she tried like hell not to think about it too much.

Quinn's eyebrows shot up. 'How on earth did you come up with that conclusion?' He laughed and picked up the bag of sour-cream-and-onion potato chips.

'You said it was one of your favorite things to do with a beautiful naked woman.' She grabbed the chip bag from him and pulled it open. 'One can only assume that it is a common occurrence with you.' Bonni bit down viciously on a chip, feeling a growing jealousy. She hated that emotion and was shocked it had decided to rear its ugly head when she'd only met this man less than twelve hours ago. 'I love chips. But I've not been able to find ketchup chips in the States.' She gave him a smirk and popped a few more in her mouth.

Quinn gave her a look, and she knew he could see through

her transparent attempt to change the subject. 'Listen, breakfast in bed is one of my favorite things to do. You know, sitting in bed, with the television on, or reading a book, while snacking on food, it's nice and lazy. And ketchup chips sound disgusting.' Quinn made a face and reached for a chocolate bar.

Bonni gasped. 'Shut your face! They are not disgusting. They are one of the many things that make Canada so unique. You should try poutine, it's to die for! But eating in bed is messy.'

He shrugged. 'I don't really understand the draw to that flavor. Or to chips in general, actually. My weakness is sweet stuff.' Quinn held out the chocolate bar, offering her some, but she shook her head, clutching her chips tighter. He took a huge bite. 'Caramel is my favorite. And I disagree. Eating in bed is just fine.' He waggled his eyebrows at her. 'It can be fun too. Pretty sure we could live off each other for a week.'

Bonni laughed, fully knowing what he was referring to. 'Yes, eating in bed can be quite delectable, fun and *pleasurable* ...' She reached for a glass of water on the bedside table to sooth her suddenly dry throat and took a sip before continuing. 'But I maintain that eating food in bed deserves a change of sheets afterwards. I will agree about caramel, though. I think, of all the candy flavors, that one's the best. But I don't like anything with nuts.'

'Are you allergic to nuts?' Quinn balled up the candy-bar wrapper and tossed it into the pile of junk food in front of them and grabbed another bar.

'No, I'm not allergic. I just don't like how they get in my teeth. And I usually get an upset stomach afterwards.' Bonni shuffled through the pile of food on the bed until she found Skittles. 'Oh, I like these! The tart sweetness makes me pucker.'

Quinn chuckled. 'I've never had that problem with nuts. Some people's bodies have weird idiosyncrasies.' He shook his head. 'I don't have any food allergies, but I start sneezing whenever spring rolls around.'

'Seasonal allergies can bother me too. Can't go anywhere without popping a decongestant.' Bonni poured some Skittles into her hand. 'I like the purple ones best. That's my favorite color. Want some?' she asked, holding out her hand.

He lifted her hand to his mouth. Keeping eye contact with her, he reached his tongue out and licked a few Skittles off her palm.

Bonni could have died as she watched his tongue lap her hand and a bunch of candies disappeared between his even white teeth. She cleared her throat when he sat back with a satisfied expression on his face.

'Uhm ... okay. Eating out of the palm of my hand – interesting.' Bonni pressed her thighs together, shocked that she was turned on. Did he even know how sexy he – *it* – was, the way he'd licked the candies right out of her hand?

'That's how you eat Skittles.' Quinn reached for a big Snickers bar and waved it in front of her. 'Now for some nuts.'

Bonni curled her lip and shook her head. 'See, I would never choose one of those. I won't be kissing you for a while.'

He froze in the action of opening the wrapper and stared down at the candy bar thoughtfully. 'Like, no kissing on the mouth? Are other areas of my body still on the table, so to speak?' He waggled his eyebrows at her again, and she reached behind her to grab a pillow, whacking him with it.

Quinn wrestled it away from her, copping a feel in the process, and suddenly she was breathless from more than just the exertion. Pretending that she didn't care that she had lost the pillow, she reached for a bag of ripple chips and held them up. 'Now this – nectar of the gods. They would be even better with a nice sour-cream dip.'

'I'm really loving this getting-to-know-you bit we're doing this morning.' Quinn smiled, and Bonni returned it. 'Food is the universal language. Next to sex, of course.'

'I thought math was.' She inspected a chip. 'I like the curly ones.' She reached out her tongue and placed the chip on it, liking how focused Quinn was on the action. 'And yes, I'm learning a lot about you.' She took a long drink of the water and put it back down on the table. 'Just don't get any crumbs in the sheets, or you'll be sleeping alone.'

Quinn furrowed his brows and made a show of patting the bed. The covers were pulled to his hips, concealing the most scrumptious part of him from her gaze. 'Hmm, I don't get the issue; nor do I see any problems. And who are you, anyway, the princess with the pea?'

He met Bonni's gaze with a fiery look and her belly tumbled over again. The last thing she had ever anticipated was to be sitting here, naked, in bed with a gorgeous and equally naked man, especially a man like him. Not something you'd expect to happen on any given day.

'"The Princess and the Pea", eh? You know what, I think I must be.' Bonni nodded. 'I'm able to find every crumb or prickly thing in my sheets. So I'm a bit anal about my bed and like it just so: clean, with fresh sheets and pluffy pillows.' Bonni inspected another curly chip.

'So what is a pluffy pillow?' Quinn inquired.

'A pillow that's a cross between puffy and fluffy ... so, pluffy. Anyway, don't change the subject.'

'I'm not, but whoa now, that's a tall order.' Bonni looked up at Quinn and, even though he was smiling at her, somehow she suddenly felt high maintenance. 'You don't like these tumbled-up sheets, the sheets that are evidence of our passionate lovemaking? Come on, food is fun, and all this is still in the package, I might add. I kinda like it tossed all over the bed.' He was teasing her, and his playful tone and the genuine look in his eyes relieved her anxiety about her feelings from a moment before. She really liked this easy banter they had already developed a habit of falling in to.

Bonni raised her hand and pointed her finger at him. 'As long as there are no crumbs in the bedsheets. Or pet hair. I dated a guy who let his dog sleep in his bed. Never. Again.'

'Noted, my princess, for the future.'

Her heart beat a little harder at the words 'the future'. She felt ridiculously excited at the possibility that there might be a future for them, even though she'd just met him last night. There was something intriguing about Quinn that made her a little receptive to the possibility that this might go beyond a one-night stand. Although the idea had occurred to her before, the full impact of it hadn't really crossed her mind . . . until now. She gazed at him, comfortable in his presence. She was beginning to think that she could discover the heart of him, and could show him herself.

'I have never been referred to as a princess, so I'll have to ponder that for a little bit. But does that mean you shall do my bidding as one does for a princess? Especially since you are already eating out of my hand?' She wiggled her fingers teasingly and he grabbed her hand to nibble at her fingertips before pressing a kiss to her palm.

'Aren't all girls princesses at some point? And –' he popped a piece of non-nutty chocolate into his mouth before continuing – 'I can be persuaded to do some bidding . . . depends on the kind.'

'Uhm, well . . .' This conversation was taking on more seductive tones, and something flared low in her abdomen. How could it not when she was naked in bed with this gorgeous man? '. . . Maybe some girls are princesses. But I've never thought of myself as a princess. I'm more of the rough-and-tumble type. A tomboy.'

Quinn reached out and caught her wrist. He pulled her easily across the rumpled sheets and on to his chest. Their treasure trove of junk food scattered across the foot of the bed and some fell on to the floor.

'Well, rough and tumble, princess or not, crumbs in the bed or military corners on the sheets, I like you here, in my arms, naked and in my bed.'

Bonni drew in a ragged breath and wrapped her arms around his neck, pressing her body to his. The merest touch of him aroused her, and she draped her leg over his thigh.

'I might just be able to get used to this kind of decadence. Eating in bed turned into a whole lot more than I anticipated. Maybe I can grow to like it a little more and not be so fussy.'

'I bet you can.' Quinn's hands trailed down her spine, coming to rest at the small of her back.

Bonni rose up and caught his mouth with hers. Their breathing mingled and she tasted the chocolatey caramel on his tongue. The crinkle of candy wrappers serenaded them and Bonni forgot about everything except Quinn, and satisfying a different kind of hunger.

Chapter 9

Something stirred Bonni, waking her from the deepest slumber. Normally a light sleeper, she'd crashed hard after their night of sex. Here she was, waking from the most refreshing sleep she'd had since – oh, *ever* – and without having to resort to her sleeping pills. What kind of magic did Quinn possess?

Stretching her body, she was languid, content after being so thoroughly worked over. She turned to her side and watched Quinn in the gloom. He was on his back, breathing deep and steady. The white top sheet was pulled up to his waist, stark in the dimly lit room.

Bonni raised her hand and hesitated a moment before lightly touching his shoulder, enjoying the feel of his skin under hers. She smiled, glad her friends had been so generous with the condoms. She knew every inch of him now and was confident that she could reduce him to a puddle in thirty seconds flat. When he stirred and raised his arm Bonni tucked herself into the groove of him, dropping her arm across his firm belly as he snuggled her tight to him.

'You're awake,' he murmured sleepily, not opening his eyes.

'Just,' she whispered into him. 'It's still dark.'

She ran her hand up him, his chest hair tickling her palm. His heart pounded steadily beneath her fingers.

'Mmm . . . I could use more sleep. You've worn me out.' He pulled her into a bear hug.

Bonni sighed, not having felt this satisfied in such a long time. She was lingering in that twilight of nearly awake but also dozing when the sound of the shower running made her realize that Quinn was no longer in bed with her.

No longer relaxed, Bonni began to worry about an exit strategy. Were the rules different for a vacation fling than for a regular one-night stand? Should she be making a discreet exit while Quinn was in the shower? She'd like to see him again but, in their haze of lust and passion, they'd never discussed the boundaries of their relationship. Could you even call what they had a relationship?

Before she had time to work herself up too much Quinn came out of the bathroom with a towel wrapped around his hips and his hair wet. She feasted her eyes on him. He was a sight that made her body insta-react. *Maybe I could lure him back to bed.*

She sat up and didn't bother to hold the sheet. It seemed silly now, after the escapades of last night. It fell to her hips and exposed her breasts to him.

'Trying to tempt me?' Quinn asked, as he ran his fingers through his hair.

'Always.' She smiled. 'Where are you off to so early?'

'First round of the tournament.'

Bonni furrowed her brows. 'Tournament?'

Quinn had been grabbing clothes from the closet but stopped to face her. 'I guess we didn't get much further than the candy in the "get-to-know-you" portion of last night. I'm a professional poker player and the Bellagio is hosting one of the biggest tournaments of the year. Qualifiers are happening over the next couple of days.'

'Oh.' Bonni felt a little uneasy, hearing he was a professional gambler.

'Something wrong?' He'd been about to drop the towel, but at the tone of her voice he readjusted it tighter on his hips instead.

A gambler and a cop? Yeah, there was something wrong with that pairing. But this was a vacation fling, possibly even just a one-night stand. He had his life, she had hers, and they'd only meet between the sheets. Bonni had absolutely no reason to be upset that their professions weren't compatible. Right?

She stretched her arms above her head, knowing it was a seductive move and that, if he could resist that, then she would understand how important his poker tournament was to him. 'Well, I was hoping for one more round before we went our separate ways.'

Quinn sat on the edge of the bed, the knot of his towel loosening. It slipped down to reveal the indentation of his hip. He smiled, and the steady look he gave her eased her mind a bit, as well as stoking her fire. 'You are extraordinarily tempting . . . you almost make me want to crawl back into bed with you.'

She looked up at him through her eyelashes and dropped her arms to the bed, leaning back a little to cause her breasts to jut out. Her movements surprised the hell out of her, as she'd never played a temptress before. Maybe it was the challenge of trying to lure him from his game, of testing him and seeing how important poker was to him. 'So let me tempt you.'

'I'd love to stay. Truly. But I have to go. They'll disqualify me if I'm not there on time.'

She could see he was fighting it, could see the passion in his eyes, and his slightly reserved nature told her he wouldn't fall prey to her. Telling herself she wasn't disappointed, Bonni nodded and reached for her clutch on the night stand. She dumped the contents on the sheets, looking for her phone so she could text her friends.

Quinn leaned over and picked up Bonni's black leather wallet. 'This isn't a very ladylike-looking wallet.'

'Who said I was a lady?' She smiled and took it from him. It wasn't a wallet; it was her police ID, holding her badge. She tucked it into her purse. She wasn't ready to tell him she was a cop. When he didn't ask any further questions, she was both relieved and a tiny bit disappointed. Maybe she wanted him to want to know more about her. Her cell had fallen and was half hidden under a fold of the sheets, and she picked it up. Quinn reached for her wrist and dragged her into his lap, and she was putty in his hands.

She liked how comfortable they were with each other. Their nakedness wasn't an issue, but then, after everything they'd done to each other last night, how was it possible to be even remotely shy?

Bonni instinctively burrowed down against his groin and he moaned a little, dropping his forehead to her shoulder. His voice muffled, he said, 'Unlock your phone.'

With a little spark of hope, she did, and the spark smoldered into a flame when he rattled off his phone number before instructing her to call him so he'd have her number too. Feeling sexy, she turned her cell's camera to selfie-mode then lifted her shoulder so he'd look up at her. Bonni held the button for a burst of shots but dropped her phone on to the bed when he kissed her.

His kiss hadn't lost its potency. Bonni deepened the kiss,

lingering in Quinn's arms, not wanting to break their embrace. Wanting to keep the kiss going. But he gently disengaged her.

'Temptress, I would gladly see this to its natural conclusion, but I do have to go. I plan on winning this tournament,' he told her.

Quinn slid out from beneath Bonni, practically dumping her on the bed. The towel provided scarce concealment for his sizeable erection. Feeling wistful that another round wouldn't be forthcoming right this second, Bonni replied, 'You're awfully confident.'

He crossed back over to his clothes and dropped the towel. She felt her mouth practically water at the sight of his firm ass. 'Damn right I'm confident.' He looked at her from under his brows as he pulled on his clothes. 'I'm good at what I do.'

She wanted to tell him: *So am I.*

'I like confidence, as long as it doesn't lead to arrogance.'

'You saying I'm arrogant now?' he teased.

Bonni shook her head. 'No, not at all. We hardly know each other, but arrogance is a trait I don't like.' She switched the conversation. 'Is the tournament open to the public?'

Quinn fished out his phone from the pocket of the pants he'd been wearing yesterday and tapped at the screen. 'To play in – no; this one is invitation only. But spectators can come watch, if that's what you meant.'

Bonni's phone buzzed with a text. Glancing down at the screen, she saw it was from Quinn. *If you and your friends come by, I promise to kick ass for you.*

She swung her legs over the side of the bed and got up. She walked to him, smiling and still not the least bit shy about her nakedness.

Quinn gave a low whistle through his teeth, reaching for her. 'You were the most wonderful, unexpected surprise last night.'

She stepped into his embrace, feeling deliciously naughty at the sensation of his clothes against her bare skin. She wrapped her arms around his neck as he pulled her tight, shivering when he ran his hand down her back to cup her bottom. He kissed her deeply and she moaned into him. They definitely had a connection. A simple kiss brewed up their passion, but Bonni wanted to be the one that broke it this time.

She looked deep into his eyes. 'That's the kind of behavior that will get you going nowhere.'

'I know, you are a temptress. I gotta go. I'm sorry.' With one last kiss, Quinn drew in a breath and stepped away from her, but he paused at the door with one last lingering look. 'Later.'

She nodded, and was hit by a shock of loneliness when the door closed behind him.

Chapter 10

After Quinn left, Bonni checked her phone for messages and scrolled through the multiple texts from her friends in their group text.

Ava xo: *I hope you had a sexy night.*

Ceez: *I hope u can barely walk! #rodehard*

Fredi: *This isn't Twitter, why do you insist on hashtagging texts?*

Ceez: *Bc Im awesome! #youwishyouwereme*

Ceez: *I see you rolling your eyes at me! #justjealous*

Ava xo: *You guys, stop! You might wake them up. Let's go get breakfast.*

Ceez: *Yaasss! Mimosas! #theluxelife*

Fredi: *Why are we texting when we are in the same room? This suite's not that big.*

Ava xo: *So B will feel included when she wakes up and know where we are!*

Ceez: *Fredi, no one forced you finish that bottle of Jack. #hangovergrumpy*

Fredi: *STOP HASHTAGGING.*

Ceez: *#no*

Ava xo: *Okay, so Bonni, we're going down to the hotel restaurant for breakfast. If you don't text us by 11 am, we'll unleash Fredi (she's SO cranky) on the front desk to get Quinn's room number and come rescue you!*

Fredi: *You know I can read that, right?*

Laughing at her friends' antics, Bonni quickly texted back, *Still alive! Gonna run to rm for quick shower + change of clothes. Will meet u downstairs.*

Bonni just had a quick elevator ride to the girls' suite, so she slipped into her dress and heels, scooped up her stuff, and headed toward the door. As she walked past the room's mirror, she paused to look at herself. She was different. A perma-smile seemed stuck to her face – she'd have to be careful she wasn't a smiling fool with the girls. Otherwise, she'd never hear the end of it

'I suppose that's what a night of good sex does to you,' Bonni told the empty room.

On her way to her suite she reflected on her night with Quinn, ignoring her friends' increasingly demanding texts for details. There was obviously so much more to get to know about Quinn. He was a professional gambler. She'd really have to give that some consideration. *Did he have a gambling problem?* Bonni had no patience for any kind of addiction. Gambling, alcohol, drugs – it didn't matter. She shook her head. She had her reasons, having been exposed to the harsh reality of addiction. No way would she ever get involved with someone she'd have to babysit.

'Stop, girl. This is just a little fling. A holiday tryst while here in Vegas. Nothing more.' She let herself in to the suite and got ready to start the day, which would begin with her friends' inquisition. Another quick elevator trip downstairs, and Bonni soon saw her friends all sitting at a table next to the railing of a café on the other side of the lobby. Weaving her way through the early-morning gamblers, she slid into the empty seat and held up a hand before they could start slinging questions at her. 'Give a girl a chance to settle down, huh? And I need a coffee. Now.'

Celia jumped up and waved for the waitress. 'Coffee, please, stat!' She sat back down and dropped her chin into her hand. 'We're dying to hear all about it.'

The waitress poured her a large coffee and Bonni watched the liquid gold flow into the mug, desperately needing a taste. She added a generous amount of cream and drew the cup between her palms, the heat warming her, as she felt suddenly chilled in the air-conditioned restaurant.

'A girl doesn't kiss and tell, you know,' she said, and took a big gulp.

Celia shook her head. 'Nope, that's a guy's line. We're your friends and you have to spill. Is he hung?'

'Celia, oh my God! You can't ask her that!'

'Shut up, Ava, you know you want to know too!'

Bonni picked up the menu and looked at the meal choices. 'Did you guys order already? Are you getting breakfast or lunch?'

Celia yanked the menu out of Bonni's hands, nearly giving her friction burns. 'Bon-Bon, I have two kids under ten and, for the next decade, my chances of a non-self-induced orgasm are pitiful. If you don't start talking, I won't be responsible for my actions.'

Ava leaned forward. 'At least tell us if he treated you right. Did you, y'know, *enjoy* yourself?'

Debriefing on guys the morning after had been the norm in college and, even now, they still texted when a date turned into a disappointment, but it didn't feel the same to talk about Quinn that way. Quinn was different. Bonni took another sip of coffee and then gave in. 'Yes, I "enjoyed" myself and Quinn is, uh, well proportioned.'

Celia squealed.

Fredi had been quiet but now she smiled at Bonni. 'I'm glad to hear that. It would have been such a disappointment if he wasn't.' She winked at her, and Bonni laughed.

Ava sighed happily and took a delicate sip from her Mimosa. 'I knew Quinn was a good guy. How was your first kiss? Was it soft and gentle or fierce and passionate?'

'It was in the elevator on the way up to his room. It was definitely in the passionate category, until these kids got on.'

'Rotten kids.' Celia drained the last of her Mimosa then twisted to flag down the waitress for another.

Bonni laughed. 'Actually, no, it gave us some breathing room. And it showed me a little bit about him. He was pretty good with them.'

Ava sighed and nodded. 'He likes kids. That's good.'

'What?' Bonni turned to her. 'Do you have us having kids now? Ava, c'mon, be serious.'

Fredi leaned forward and tried to diffuse the questioning. 'Bonni's right. This is a fling. Nothing more.'

The waitress came with Celia's Mimosa. They ordered food, and Ava waited until the waitress left before she asked, 'So are you going to see him again?'

'Oh, no, wait, we're not done talking about the sex.' Celia tapped the table demandingly.

'Sorry to disappoint, but I'm not going to give you a play-by-play, you can forget about that.'

'But we want one,' Celia insisted.

Bonni shook her head, and the image of Quinn, firmly

between her thighs, flashed through her mind. Heat warmed her cheeks and she ducked her face down so the others wouldn't see.

'Holy shit!' Celia cried out. 'You're blushing. Bonni, I don't remember if I've ever seen you blush. It must've been really good. How many times did you come?'

'For the love of God, Celia, only dogs can hear you at that pitch. If she doesn't want to talk about it, she doesn't want to talk about it!'

An awkward silence fell on the table at Fredi's outburst. Then Bonni held up her hand and flashed *four* on her fingers. Ava gasped, and Celia squealed again. Fredi just huffed and said, 'I'm running to the bathroom.'

After Fredi left the table Bonni looked at Ava and Celia. 'Okay, what did I miss?'

'So, we left the club around 2 a.m. in the cab Quinn got for us—'

Bonni interrupted Ava's retelling. 'Wait. Quinn got you a cab?'

Celia answered as she idly doodled in the condensation on her Mimosa glass. 'Yeah. I guess he's a regular at the club, so he made arrangements with that security guard to make sure our drunk asses weren't roaming around Vegas at dark o'clock.'

'I had no idea.' A wave of softness swept Bonni that Quinn would do such a thing for three women he had just met.

Ava continued, 'It was really a sweet gesture. Anyway, we'd just stumbled into the suite when Fredi's boss at DWD called her on her cell. Apparently, some bride who's getting married next week started harassing them about the lace on her train or something and they wanted Fredi to fly home to fix it. She told them no. There was this whole big argument and curse words

I've never heard before. I don't think she got much sleep last night.'

'Yep, and the whole conversation ended with a *bless your heart*.' Celia gave them a wide-eyed look and shook her head. 'Aves, you are so PG-13, if you didn't know some of those curses. I keep telling Fredi to quit and open her own studio, but no, it's never the "right time".'

They all had stubborn streaks, but Fredi was the most loyal. It took a lot to get her to walk away. Bonni finished her coffee, and the waitress came over with a pot to refill her mug. Just as she left, Fredi came back and slid into her seat, snapping her napkin back on to her lap.

Fredi asked, 'Did you answer Ava? Are you seeing Quinn again?'

Bonni, Ava and Celia glanced at each other and silently agreed to ignore Fredi's red eyes and freshly re-applied make-up. Bonni fidgeted a little and then answered, 'Well, he did give me his number. And invited us to watch him work.'

'He gave you his number? I knew it wasn't just a one-night stand!' Ava nodded her head.

'Watch him work? Is he a stripper? Oh, we are *so* going. We need the check,' Celia announced.

Ava and Celia were speaking over each other and Bonni had to grab Celia's arm to stop her from enthusiastically calling over the waitress. 'No, he's a poker player. There's a tournament at the Bellagio.'

Both women visibly deflated. Ava said, 'That's not a real job, is it?'

Celia agreed. 'And what are you supposed to watch? A bunch of men sitting a table trying to be the alpha male and attempting to out-bluff each other?'

Now it was Bonni's turn to be deflated. She hadn't realized

until now that she had been hoping to convince her friends to check out the tournament. Her body remembered quite nicely how good she and Quinn were together. She hungered for him almost as much as for the bacon and eggs she'd ordered.

Fredi regarded her thoughtfully for a beat then said, 'You want to go, don't you?'

'No, no,' Bonni said, probably not fooling any of them, 'This is a girls' trip.'

Now it was the other three's turn to silently communicate. Then Celia said, 'Since we didn't know when you'd leave your love den, we made our own plans for the morning. Fredi and I are going to hit the casino and Ava is taking a tour of the locations where famous movies were filmed. You totally have time to watch him do his thing.'

She seriously had the best friends ever. 'Are you guys sure? I don't want you to think I'm ditching you.'

Celia airily waved her Mimosa in the air. 'Bitch, please.'

Ava was dreamily staring off into space, probably trying to figure out what their couple name would be, and Fredi just smirked at her. Bonni said, 'Okay, so I'll go check out Quinn and his tournament, but I'm also going to book us spa treatments for this afternoon. My treat, of course.'

Fredi said, 'I'm not going to argue with you. See if you can book a masseuse that gives a "happy ending".'

Celia bounced in her seat. 'Yesss, totally. I need a "happy ending" too!'

Ava remarked wistfully, 'I bet Quinn and Bonni are going to have a happy ending.'

Bonni looked at Ava, trying to figure out if she was making an innuendo or if she was serious. You could never tell with her friend. Before Celia could say something outrageous, the waitress brought over their food.

'Oh, thank God. Okay, no more sex talk.'

Ava happily dived into her food while Celia and Fredi shot Bonni looks of betrayal. She didn't care, though, as she bit into a crispy strip of bacon. Sometimes a girl's gotta do what a girl's gotta do.

'Bonni, don't think you can distract me with tales of a hot masseuse.' Celia was clearly on a mission.

'What? I'm not distracting you. We're going for a massage later, right?'

'Yeah, but that doesn't mean we don't need to talk more about the sex,' Celia said, around a mouth loaded with scrambled eggs.

'Didn't your mother ever tell you not to speak with your mouth full?' Bonni teased her friend, glad that she was enjoying herself and being silly.

'Yup, same thing I say to my kids too. But they're not here. No kids! Yay! So rules don't apply. Plus, my mom isn't here.' She took another big forkful of eggs and her cheeks puffed out like a chipmunk's. 'Now I really have my mouth full. Only it's not what I really want to have a mouth full of.' Celia swallowed and then cackled like a hyena.

Bonni burst out laughing. So did Ava and Fredi.

'Holy shit, I haven't heard that laugh in years!' Fredi said between giggles.

'Celia, you know that laugh is enough to twist us inside out. Good God, I love your crazy old laugh.' Bonni was crying, she laughed so hard, and had to hold her stomach.

They had just begun to calm down when Ava did her infamous snort, which sent them all once again into peals of laughter.

'This is going to be one great trip,' Bonni said.

'For sure.' Fredi took a deep breath before stirring her fruit salad, looking for the choicest bits of melon.

'I'm so glad we are doing this,' Ava agreed, cutting her pancakes into four quadrants, her fork and knife making little clicking noises against the plate.

'Oh, hang on. My phone's ringing.' Celia stood up and pulled her cell from the back pocket of her jeans.

She let out a cry of delight and held it up to show her friends. 'It's my kids. They're calling me!' A huge smile lit up her face. Gone was the wild party woman and in her place was a mom. A mom who loved and missed her kids.

Celia tapped the screen, and the biggest, happiest, most loving expression crossed her face when she laid eyes on her beloved children. Bonni's mouth quirked into a half-smile. If you'd asked her ten years ago where Celia would be at the end of the decade, it wouldn't be here, but Bonni privately thought that Celia's kids made her the best possible person.

'Oh, my babies. How are you doing? I miss you guys.' She blew kisses into the screen, and Bonni heard exaggerated kisses coming through the phone.

These kids really loved their mom.

'Are you FaceTimeing?' Bonni asked, craning her neck to see. She was Jilly's godmother.

'Yes,' Celia answered, and turned her phone around so everyone could see. 'Say hi to my babies!'

'Hey, Colin! Hi, Jilly. Are you guys having fun?' Bonni asked them, as she blew them a kiss.

'Hi, Auntie Bons!' Jilly said, and Colin waved at her.

'Wow, are you guys growing up! I have to come for a visit soon.' She suddenly realized how much time had gone by. This was what happened when you dedicated your life to saving the world. The world moved on without you.

Ava grabbed Celia's hand and turned the phone toward her.

'Hello, my two favorite little monsters. I'm so happy to see your beautiful faces. Oh, but wow, you certainly don't look like little people anymore. You're getting all grown up.' Ava gave them a pout and then a bright smile. Colin and Jilly laughed, clearly thrilled to be told they looked all grown up.

'You certainly are looking like the handsome young man, Master Colin. And look at your hair, Miss Jilly, it's getting so long.' Fredi also blew them a kiss, and smiled. Bonni watched her and was a little surprised at the wistful expression Fredi momentarily let slip across her face. That made Bonni a bit sad. Fredi never gave any indication she was wanting kids, let alone to be married.

It made Bonni wonder if she herself was mother material. She'd never even thought about it before. To have another human being completely and utterly dependent on you . . . It was a rather frightening and exciting concept.

The kids giggled and jockeyed for position in the camera screen. They argued a little bit. 'Hey, you two!' Celia said. 'Stop fighting. I can't referee you from here. Where's your dad?' As soon as Celia said the word 'dad', Bonni saw her shoulders tense up.

'He's in his office,' Jilly advised. The little girl was the oldest, at nearly eight. She wore a battered soccer jersey and her blonde hair, the same color as her mother's, was pulled back in a haphazard ponytail with strands flying out all over the place.

'Imma go now, Mom, got a game to play.' Colin had just turned six. While Jilly was happiest outdoors, Colin liked technology, whether it was his gaming system or a book on his iPad.

'Wait, Colin, not yet. I want to talk to you a little longer.'

'Aww, Mom!' Colin crossed his arms and pouted, his joy at

seeing his mother diminished by the lure of a video game going unplayed.

'Quiet, Colin! Mom, we're having fun. Daddy bought us some new movies for our sleepover and Grandma Kate came over to make us tuna and tater tots. Are you having fun?' Jilly asked.

Kate was the dickwad's mother, and she and Celia had never gotten along. The thought of Kate having access to her kids without her there made Celia's free hand clench into a fist, and she tilted her face down to avoid having her kids see her expression. Bonni nipped the phone out of Celia's hand to give her friend some time to recover.

'Of course your mom is having fun. We're all having fun. In fact, we are just finishing up with our breakfast.'

'What did you have? Pancakes and bacon?' Colin asked.

'I had bacon and eggs, your mom had scrambled eggs, and do you know what?'

'What?' They asked in unison.

'She was talking with her mouth full.'

'Mom, you get mad at us for that!' Colin yelled into the phone.

'Say goodbye to my friends, kids,' Celia said, loud enough for them to hear. 'I want to talk to you for a little while by myself now.' She held the phone up for everyone to see. They all waved and gave a chorus of goodbyes as Celia turned it back to her as the kids sang out their goodbyes through the phone.

Celia stood and picked up her bag. 'I'm just gonna go and talk to them for a little while over there.' She pointed to the other side of the lobby, where some chairs were tucked away in a corner.

Bonni watched Celia walk away, looking into her phone with that big and loving smile etched on her face. She really was an awesome mom, and she totally deserved these few days away. Bonni sensed she had feelings of guilt at leaving her kids behind, but Celia also needed to take care of herself. Once she'd said her goodbyes to her babies, Bonni was convinced Party Celia would be back with a vengeance.

Chapter 11

Quinn wanted to focus on the cards. Good God, he'd had a hard time leaving the suite. Memories floated across his mind: Bonni sitting naked in the bed, her breasts begging to be kissed. Her soft moans last night as he discovered her secret spots. Her responsiveness to his touch. The sounds she made when she orgasmed . . . how the hell was he supposed to focus? But he had to.

The only thing he could do was push her out of his mind. Forget how sexy she was, and how wonderful she looked, lying all caught up in the sheets on his bed. He needed to concentrate. He could fuck up the first elimination round, and that would be a disaster.

Quinn lifted the edge of his cards and kept his face blank. Lady Luck was being kind to him today. If he screwed it up, he'd only have himself to blame. From behind his dark glasses and under the shadow from the brim of his baseball cap, he watched the other players. Unlike the others, who chose a more casual style or dressed to conceal their tells, he chose to shield his face only with a cap and sunglasses, maintaining a more professional appearance with tailored slacks and a crisp shirt, open at the neck. He pulled the brim of his cap a little lower, casting his face deeper in shadow. Some tournaments, he'd forgo the hat entirely, but he didn't completely trust himself to keep his emotions hidden today.

He had pocket aces. Quinn rolled a chip along his knuckles, for drama, then put it down. He pushed his entire stack of chips into the center of the table, and the crowd watching gasped. He was all in. Two players threw their cards down, folding, and his last opponent called. He and Quinn revealed their hands, and the crowd erupted. Relief swept through him. He'd won.

He let out a big breath, sat back in the chair, stretching his cramped body, and looked around for his brother, Landon, seeing him in the back corner. He stood up, stretched again, and indicated to his brother to meet him outside the casino after Quinn had finished the necessary paperwork.

'One down,' he told Landon. 'I was warned this was going to be a tough tournament.'

Landon clapped him on the back. 'You had it, but what was distracting you?'

Quinn was surprised that Landon had picked up on it. He shook his head. 'Nothing. Didn't get much sleep last night.'

He wasn't ready to tell Landon about Bonni. He'd get on his ass about her. Landon always expected women to have hidden agendas. If he found out about Bonni distracting him with her sexiness, Landon would immediately assume she was a gold-digger planted by one of Quinn's competitors. His brother eyed him for a moment and then let it go.

'I'm glad I was able to fly out for this. It's been too long since we've hung out,' Landon said, and checked his watch.

With Landon established in San Francisco, and Quinn

basically a nomad, following the games, they mainly kept in touch through video-chatting and on-the-fly texts. Quinn nodded. 'You got that right. Let's grab a bite.'

Landon looked around then pointed to a classy-looking restaurant. 'Definitely in the mood for steak.'

As they headed across the floor, Quinn found himself scanning the crowd. Checking the faces . . . for her. It didn't go unnoticed.

'Who are you looking for, Quinn?' Landon's tone was suspicious.

Shit. 'No one.'

'Don't bullshit me. You are clearly checking out the crowds. I know you're not in debt to loan sharks because I manage your portfolio. Is it a deranged fan? Dammit, Quinn, I told you that you should hire a bodyguard.'

Quinn grunted. 'It's not a deranged fan. I don't know where you get these ideas, numb-nuts. I'm not as popular as you think I am.' He slid his phone out of his pocket to check again if Bonni had texted him, trying to hide the motion from Landon.

'Excuse me if I want to avoid having to pay ransom for your stupid ass. So, if it's not a stalker, it's a woman. Same thing, I guess.' The hostess at the podium of the restaurant raised her eyebrow at that, but Landon flashed a smile and the woman noticeably thawed, leading them to a table with a view of the casino via one-way glass.

Quinn picked up his menu, hoping his annoying older brother would let it go, but Lady Luck had clearly abandoned him now that the poker game was over. 'So who is she? She must have been pretty good to have you knotted up at a game.'

The implication that the only reason he was interested in

Bonni was her skill in bed didn't sit right with him. Okay, true, they haven't had any in-depth conversations yet, but he'd seen the care and concern she'd shown for her friends last night, and enjoyed their banter in the elevator and while snacking. He'd been hoping she'd come see him play because he wanted to know her beyond the bedroom.

'Fuck off, asshole. I'm hoping to see her again tonight.'

'Whoa, two nights in a row? Now that's different.'

His brother was giving him a hard time. And Landon continued to bust his chops throughout their appetizers and steaks. Quinn let it roll off his back (his brother had so few joys in his life) and debated whether he should text Bonni.

The two brothers finished off their steaks. Landon put down his fork and placed his napkin beside the plate. 'That hit the spot.' Sitting back in the chair, he rested his arm on the back of the seat beside him.

'How did you manage to get the time away?' Quinn asked his brother.

'I'm CEO, I can do whatever I like.' Landon smiled. 'But Mom was also on my case about finding a date for her next charity gala. I decided a little vacation would do us both good.' He reached for his glass and finished off the Italian red.

'How long you staying for?' Quinn checked his phone again. Still no text from Bonni.

'Thought I'd stay and watch you win.'

Quinn smiled. 'I figured.'

Something caught his eye through the restaurant windows. He squinted and searched the throng shuffling by. Then he saw her, and his breath stuck in his lungs. Just like last night, the crowd seemed to part and a light shown down, illuminating her. His reverence for Lady Luck aside, Quinn wasn't particularly superstitious, but this was the second time he'd seen

Bonni among a mass of people, and everyone around her faded to grey. He had to admit it felt like some kind of sign.

'I'll be right back.' He grabbed his phone and bolted from the chair.

'Where are you going? Are you sticking me with the check, jackass?'

Quinn heard Landon, but didn't bother to answer his brother as he rushed out of the restaurant before he lost sight of Bonni.

But, by the time he'd got out to the crowd, she was gone.

'Damnit!' Quinn searched for her dark head. Weaving in and out, he picked up his pace until he saw her ahead. Quinn smiled at the rush of emotion that filled his chest. Just then, his phone – finally – buzzed.

Hi, it's Bonni. I was going to surprise you at the tournament, but then I thought maybe that would distract you or something. I don't know if you get breaks between rounds or whatever, but let me know if it's still okay if I stop by.

Her head was bent over her phone and she stood partially blocked by a pillar. Approaching her, he used his phone to reply: *Turn around.*

When he was close enough he reached out and grabbed her arm.

She whirled to face him, her hand raised, and he was pretty sure that, if he hadn't dodged, she would have punched him.

'Hey. It's me,' he said, feeling a little foolish.

'Holy shit, Quinn, what the hell! You don't go around grabbing women from behind! Didn't your mother ever teach you that?'

The frustration in her voice was a new element to her, and he decided he much preferred her soft moans of passion.

'I'm sorry, I shouldn't have done that,' he said, giving her his most charming smile.

Bonni rolled her shoulders slowly, allowing the tension to seep from her body. She lightly swatted him on the arm. 'Don't do it again.'

He caught her hand and entwined their fingers. At last she smiled back, and gave his hand a gentle squeeze. 'I thought you were in the tournament?'

'It's finished. Done a while ago now.' Quinn felt his phone buzzing in his pocket and knew it was his brother, wondering where he was. Landon could wait.

'Really? I thought they took forever. Like an all-day affair – you know, as seen on TV.'

He shook his head. 'Sometimes it can, but this one was quick. It didn't take long. I won.' Quinn wasn't in the habit of bragging about a win in a qualifier – it felt too much like he might jinx the tournament – but he wanted to impress Bonni.

'Oh my God, Quinn, that's awesome! Congratulations! What happens next?' Bonni moved in to give him a congratulatory hug, and he wrapped an arm around her waist before she could step back.

'Next qualifier is bright and early tomorrow. So, do you have plans for tonight?'

Bonni draped her arms over his shoulders and leaned into him. 'We're doing spa treatments in about an hour, but I'm not a hundred per cent sure about tonight. We've talked about going to a show, but no one has decided yet.'

Over her shoulder, Quinn saw Landon walk toward them, glancing down at his phone. Bastard was probably tracking him through the Find Your Friends app. Turning it on had been a condition Landon had insisted on before he agreed to manage Quinn's personal portfolio. He was such a worrywart.

'Dine and ditching your own brother. Just for that, you're paying me back for the whole thing now.' Landon gave Quinn a pointed look. He turned his attention to Bonni. 'And who do we have here?'

Quinn could feel Bonni stiffen up. She didn't wait for Quinn to introduce them. Stepping back, she forced him to release her and reached out a hand to Landon. 'Bonni Connolly.'

He savored the fact that he now knew her last name, which momentarily distracted him from Landon grasping Bonni's hand and attempting to smolder at her. 'Landon Bryant, this shithead's brother. Pleased to meet you.' His eyebrows rose. 'That's a firm handshake you have there, Bonni.'

Okay, that was enough of that. Quinn shot his brother a murderous glare, and the bastard smirked before Bonni managed to tug her hand free. She looked between the two men. 'Sorry, but I don't see a resemblance.'

He'd been hearing that all his life. While they shared a similar build, Quinn took after his father while Landon resembled their mother. 'No, Landon didn't inherit the family's rugged good looks, but we let him stick around.'

Bonni smiled at him while Landon flipped him off behind her back. His brother got his revenge, though. 'So, Bonni, what are you doing now? I'd love to hear about how you and Quinn met.'

Before Quinn could cut off that line of questioning, Bonni was explaining about meeting up with her friends. 'Oh, you have time, then? You must let Quinn and I treat you to this wonderful patisserie in the hotel. They have simply delicious macarons.'

Landon began to usher Bonni away, and she shot Quinn a

look over her shoulder. His hopes of sequestering Bonni for some private time to explore the connection between them disappeared. Quinn stalked after his brother and his woman, wondering how mad his mother would be if he took steps to become an only child.

Chapter 12

The spa music was lovely. It soothed and calmed her. Bonni had hoped to spend an hour or so staring at Quinn while he did his thing, but instead she'd had the most sinful pastries while Quinn and his brother traded jabs at each other. Landon had never completely relaxed, though, and Bonni could tell he wasn't entirely sold on her. He'd asked a lot of questions about what she did for a living and where she was from, but she had deflected them as best as she could. She had glanced quickly at Quinn to see if he was wondering as well, but he'd been busy inspecting his pastry.

Quinn had walked her to the entrance of the hotel, and the taxi stand, but before they exited he pulled her into a secluded alcove and kissed her senseless. If it hadn't been for the girls texting her, she might still be in his arms. Bonni promised to text him later, once her plans with the girls were finalized. Thinking about his kisses made her muscles melt, and her anxiety about leaving Quinn subsided. It surprised her how much she longed to be with him; it was something she wasn't used to.

A man had never thrown her off her game so much before. This was new, and she was trying to figure it out. Bonni stared at the hot, bubbling water foaming around her feet. It felt glorious. Almost as good as Quinn massaging her feet last night. He certainly had the touch.

She almost moaned aloud, thinking about how sweetly they fitted together. Their bodies matched perfectly and . . . *stop torturing yourself, Bonni.* She shook her head and did her best to put him out of her mind.

'Earth to Bonni.' A vague voice reached through her thoughts, and a poke in the arm nearly made her jump out of her skin. It seemed she wasn't doing so good at focusing on the here and now.

She glanced up to find Fredi snapping her fingers. 'Bonni! Please rejoin us on Planet Earth.'

'Sorry, I was thinking about something and enjoying the soak.' Bonni's toes curled beneath the water as she looked up to find her friend staring at her.

'Obviously. I've been talking away about this consultation I had with this Bridal Bitch and you haven't said a word.' Fredi sounded frustrated and Bonni felt bad.

'I'm sorry. Again. I'm being a bad friend. My mind has just been busy.' She pushed herself up in the chair a little higher and began fretting about how torn she was between hanging out with her friends and being with a man she barely knew. These were her girls, the sisters of her heart, who she barely got to see now that they were scattered across North America. Could she really sacrifice time with them for a vacation fling – for Quinn?

'Your preoccupation wouldn't have anything to do with the sexy man that swept you off your feet last night, would it? Did he give you a standing "O" when you saw him this afternoon?' Fredi winked.

Bonni turned bright red and tilted her head to the side. '*Seriously?*'

'Yes, seriously. Having sex in public can add a little spice to the proceedings. Anyway, I can tell you are out in Never-Never Land.' Fredi's bluntness was always refreshing, even if it was annoying at times.

Bonni glanced at Ava and Celia. They were relaxing in their chairs, cucumbers resting over their eyes and ear buds in. Both of them were very snobbish when it came to music. Ava was probably listening to the latest Broadway-hit musical soundtrack or the most up-to-the-minute pop-country act and, judging by the tapping of Celia's fingers, she was blissed out to classic rock.

She turned to Fredi and leaned over. 'I know this is supposed to be a vacation fling, but I can't get him out of my head,' she admitted, something she hadn't thought she'd be able to do.

Fredi raised her eyebrows. 'That didn't take long. Does he have magic hands or something?' Her crystal-blue eyes narrowed.

'You have no idea. I swear.' Bonni let her head fall back and sighed.

'Uh-oh. Are you hooked?' The deeply concerned tone in Fredi's voice clashed with the soothing spa music coming from the carefully concealed speakers.

Bonni tilted her face to look at Fredi, 'I can't believe it. Me. The epitome of independence. I spend my life surrounded by men – some really hot, really built men – and meh. But one look at Quinn across a crowded dance floor . . .' She waved her hands in an agitated motion. 'This is straight out of those sappy movies Ava likes so much. What am I supposed to do with this . . . this . . . whatever it is?'

Fredi leaned on the arm of the chair. 'Look. Stop being hard on yourself. Roll with it. Enjoy the moment and don't think about where it's going. Because it's likely going nowhere. It's a fling . . .in Vegas. Just don't fall in love, get pregnant or catch an STD. Not everything in Vegas stays in Vegas. Most importantly, enjoy yourself and have some fun. Take a break from saving society from itself. You only live once.'

Bonni laughed and reached out to take Fredi's hand. 'You do have a way of putting things in perspective. But I feel guilty spending time with him when I came here to be with you guys.'

'*Looook.*' Fredi emphasized the word and pointed at Ava and Celia. 'Do you think those two would hesitate if they were in your shoes? We'd have to hog-tie Ava to keep her from rushing to the altar, and Dickhead's done such a number on Celia, if any man could actually make her feel sexy and desirable again, I'd probably loan him my handcuffs.'

Bonni snickered. 'When did you get handcuffs, you kinky thing, you?'

Fredi gave Bonni a mischievous look which made her laugh even harder.

Bonni waved her hand. 'Okay. Let's figure out what we're going to do tonight and then I'll text Quinn.'

Fredi picked up her phone and began tapping at the screen. 'No worries, B, we'll make sure you get your Quinn fix.'

Bonni lifted a shoulder. 'Do you have to phrase it like that?'

Her friends knew how she felt about substance abuse and addiction. Her older brother had started drinking heavily in college and then started experimenting with drugs. Their parents had managed to get him help before he destroyed his life. Bonni didn't mind cutting loose and partying with her friends on occasion, but she preferred to be the designated driver.

Gambling was another activity that was fun once in a while, but it was a slippery slope and could easily take over. Her discomfort at Quinn's profession rose to the surface. It seemed hypocritical to be judging him for gambling when she had won that money playing the slots but, to her, it was different. Just a stroke of luck – being in the right place at the right time. But Quinn, his livelihood depended on the turn of a card. What happened when the cards were against him? But she remembered the thrill she'd gotten when she'd won, how much she'd been enjoying having the extra money to spoil her friends, so maybe she could understand. She sighed and decided she couldn't think about it anymore.

Fredi chucked a magazine at Celia and it thunked against her knee, barely avoiding falling into her footbath. Celia hardly reacted and said, 'Fuck off, Fredi. I'm currently on a beach with a strapping young man named Antonio, who is feeding me grapes, and I'm not worrying about how to replace the cleats Jilly outgrew. She's such a tomboy.'

Ava took out her ear buds and peeled off the cucumber slices. Lifting her glass of wine, she said, 'This is just divine. Not a spreadsheet in sight, just pampering and my best friends.'

Reluctantly, Celia pulled out her ear buds too. 'Goodbye, Antonio.' Balling up her cucumber slices in a tissue, she said, 'I love my kids, but it's been so great being me again and not Mom. You have no idea how much I appreciate this. The whole weekend – the spa, being with you guys.' She let out an exaggerated puff of air. 'Oh yeah, this is a heavenly break for me. Bring on the wine!' Celia held up her glass.

Bonni picked hers up and they all did a cheers. Fredi said, 'So, I don't know how Antonio will stack up, but I got us tickets to *Thunder Down Under*. The 7 p.m, show. I figure we'll have a fabulous dinner after getting pampered and then go ogle hot Aussie men.'

Celia pumped a fist. 'I've got no problem ditching Antonio for real-life Hemsworth lookalikes.'

Ava said, 'There's this great sushi place I've heard about. Bonni, do you think Quinn might want to come?'

'While I think it's hot as hell to fantasize about Quinn being an equal opportunist, Bon-Bon might want to cut her losses now, since she doesn't like sharing.' It was hard, Bonni thought, because, on the one hand, she was glad Celia was reclaiming her spirit but, on the other, she said the most outrageous, embarrassing, things.

'You know perfectly well I meant dinner! Not that there's anything wrong with being bisexual. Is he bi, Bonni?' Bonni was too busy facepalming to answer Ava, so Fredi replied.

'Dudes, she just met him. I'm sure they haven't had the sexual preferences and kinks discussions yet. Bonni will stick with us for dinner and the show, and then she can go explore Quinn's sexual fantasies. And we're not having sushi, Aves. No one likes raw fish but you.'

Seizing the subject change, Bonni said, 'Remember when the most exotic cuisine Ava would eat was quesadillas? City life has changed our baby girl.'

Ava laughed. 'Having to accompany David on business dinners forced me to expand my palate, especially since it was free food and living in the city is expensive.'

'And how is David doing? He can certainly fill out a suit in the pictures you posted on Instagram.' Celia waggled her eyebrows.

'He and his wife are very happy, thank you. They just had the most adorable baby girl. Besides, mixing business and pleasure never works.' Ava glanced to the side before draining the rest of her wine.

Bonni changed the subject again. 'Fredi, tell me how much the tickets were and I'll cover them.'

'Part of me wants to argue, and the rest of me knows how damn stubborn you are.'

'Don't be ridiculous,' Ava insisted. 'It's not fair you—'

'I mean it, Ava.' Bonni looked pointedly at each one, giving them the fiercest cop stare. 'You guys don't spend any money. Charge whatever you can to the hotel room, and I got everything else.'

They all hesitated, looked at each other, then nodded their heads.

'Thank you.' Ava blew her a kiss.

'You're the best, Bonni, and you know how much this means to me.' Celia touched her chest above her heart and Bonni thought she saw tears glistening in her eyes.

'Love you, Bons.' Fredi reached over and squeezed her arm.

The attendants came in and did their pedicures while they chatted. Bonni was happy about how things had worked out, that she could spend time with her friends and with Quinn. Ava told a funny anecdote from her morning tour and Celia caught them up on the latest with her kids. Bonni wondered if she could convince Celia to take money for Jilly's sporting equipment before the end of the weekend. Maybe she should just order the cleats and have them sent to Celia's house.

'Ladies, please follow me, and I will show you to your respective rooms for your massages.' An attendant led the way and they all followed her down a hallway. The wonderful aroma of massage oils hung on the air.

'Ms Connolly, you are in here.'

'I can't wait. I need this.' Bonni waved goodbye to her friends and, as the door was closing behind her, she heard Celia in the hall. 'See you all later. Hey, I have a dude! Sweeeet.'

Bonni laughed, and could almost see the big smile Celia would have on her face as she checked him out.

She sat in a chair and waited for her masseuse to come in. Moments later, a mature woman entered. 'Hello, I'm Sarah.' She walked over to Bonni and gave her shoulder a squeeze with strong fingers then moved to her neck.

Oh my, this is going to be great.

'You're very tense.'

'Don't I know it.'

'Well, we can work on that. I have you for ninety minutes. You can hang your robe on that hook. Are you okay to get on the table by yourself?'

'Yes, thank you.'

'I'll be back in a moment then.'

Bonni climbed on the table and slipped under the sheet. The table was warm, and strategically placed pillows supported her body nicely. Bonni rested her face into the draped pillow and relaxed. A soft knock on the door, and Sarah came back in.

Bonni didn't want to talk and lay quietly as Sarah worked on her. Her fingers were strong and gentle, sweeping and soothing. Bonni lost track of time and fell into a trance under her hands. She thought about Quinn. The way he had touched her last night. The release of endorphins from Sarah's touch and the remembrance of the pleasure Quinn had brought her was a wicked combination. She couldn't wait to see him again, and for his hands to be on her again.

Chapter 13

The show had been just as good as advertised, and Fredi had scored them great seats.

'Those were worth every penny,' Bonni said.

'When that one guy sidled up to Ava I thought I was going to die laughing.' Celia giggled, just remembering it.

'Oh, he was *hottttt*. I swear, I got a contact high just from being near him. And the guy in the SWAT uniform! Bonni, are you holding out on us?'

'Ha, no. They grow them mighty fine in Canada, but none of the guys I work with is quite so . . . sculpted.'

Celia put her arm around Fredi and gave her a squeeze. 'How about the tuxedoed dudes? Wouldn't they make excellent arm-candy for the models of your wedding dresses?'

Fredi nodded. 'They would certainly catch any bride's attention. I don't think I've ever seen such perfect specimens of men before.' She turned to Bonni. 'What do you think? Still settled on Quinn? I think the cowboy was eyeing you from the stage.'

'Okay, enough of that already. Those guys are gorgeous,

there's no doubt about it. They are unreachable. Untouchable. And I bet they're all gay.'

'Bon-Bon, don't say that! It completely ruins the fantasy.' Celia frowned, and Bonni could tell she was thinking about it. 'Damn. Oh, well, there's always Antonio.'

'What do you say we head back to our hotel?' Bonni suggested. They agreed and found a cab to pile into.

Back at the Gladiators, Fredi announced: 'There are some gorgeous hotels on the Strip, but I've become attached to this one.'

They walked through *their* hotel. Four confident, beautiful women. Bonni wondered if the others noticed the looks they were getting. They were hot, and walking like they owned the place. Bonni was so happy for this girls' weekend away with her friends. She wanted to make sure they continued to have a great time. But Quinn was on her mind, and she checked her watch.

'What time are you meeting Quinn?' Ava asked her.

'I have about another thirty minutes.'

'Perfect, we have time to go and grab a drink or something.' Celia pointed off to the left. 'We haven't been to that place yet.'

It was packed, and they were lucky to find a row of stools at the bar.

Bonni got her phone out and set it in front of her.

'Where are you meeting him?' Celia asked, as she looked at the cocktail list.

'We haven't really decided. I told him I'd text him when we were done.'

'Why don't you have him come here?' Ava suggested.

'Good idea.' It gave her more time with her friends, and Quinn's room was right upstairs. After sending the text, she put the phone down to order a Hendricks and tonic. Just as the bartender was serving her drink, her phone chimed.

Quinn Bryant: *Yep. 10 minutes.*

'Was that him?' Ava asked her.

'Yes. It was.'

Celia clapped her hands. 'Ohhh, we're going to meet him again. How exciting.'

'You know where you're going?' Fredi asked her.

Bonni shook her head. 'No, we didn't really make plans on what we were going to do, just that we would see each other.' She looked at her friends. 'Thanks for being so understanding.'

'Of course,' Ava said. 'It isn't every day you meet someone that leaves you breathless.'

'I never said he left me breathless.'

'You didn't have to. Every time you talk about him your voice gets a little lower and I can hear the breathless.'

'Oh, come on, I do not get like that!' Bonni put her elbow on the bar.

'Uhm, yes, you do. Fredi's going to be designing your wedding dress any day now.'

Fredi rolled her eyes. 'Ava, you are the only one who constantly emails me about what you want your dress to look like.'

'I don't *constantly* email you.' Ava pouted.

Fredi mouthed *constantly* to Bonni and Celia.

'Well, I'm never getting married again. One dickhead was enough for a lifetime,' Celia declared.

Ava touched her arm. 'He was a necessary evil so you could get your babies. One day your knight in shining armor will come along.'

'I don't need a knight in shining armor. I can take care of my kids and myself and my mother, and I don't need a man in my life who thinks he knows what's best!' Celia's voice was passionate and frustrated, and tears sprang to her eyes.

'Oh, honey . . .' Bonni wrapped an arm around her friend's

shoulders and Celia dropped her head on Bonni's shoulder while Ava held her hand.

'Don't be nice to me right now. I'll really lose it if you're nice to me. And we've had such a lovely night.' Bonni's heart broke for her friend. She had no idea Celia had bottled up her feelings to this extent, and she resolved to be more present in her friend's life after the weekend was over.

'Okay. I didn't think we were going to get all maudlin.' Fredi picked up her beer and took a swig from the bottle. She put it back down and declared, 'When Bonni goes off with her Mr Right Now, Ava and I are going to try to get some action on the Where Will Celia Puke? pool.'

They all broke out into laughter. Trust Fredi to lighten the mood and get them back into party mode. She and Celia started bickering good-naturedly while Bonni took a long sip of her drink through the straw. The fine hairs on the nape of her neck prickled, and she twirled around on her barstool to see Quinn coming. Her heart did a little flip-flop and her body temp rose. He was with Landon. She quickly finished her drink and put the glass down.

'I guess somebody is here,' Fredi said, with a teasing tone in her voice.

Bonni nodded. 'And he brought somebody with him.'

Fredi turned to look. 'Holy shit! Who the hell is that?'

'That's his brother.'

Bonni watched Fredi check out Landon, a little surprised at her reaction to seeing Quinn's brother.

Ava and Celia turned around when Bonni stood up.

'He's with someone.' Ava looked at Bonni. 'Is that the brother?'

Bonni had filled them in over dinner on her bizarre coffee date with Landon and Quinn.

'Yup.'

'Is he single?' Celia asked.

'I didn't ask him his marital status when he was grilling me, sorry.'

'Well, you should have,' Celia whispered, and Bonni blinked, seeing the sudden shift in Celia's demeanor.

Very interesting. Maybe, just maybe . . . hmm. Bonni wasn't a matchmaker, as a rule, but perhaps she could make an exception. She'd keep an eye on her persons of interest and see if there was any evidence to support the potential seed of a relationship.

The closer the men got, the more nervous Bonni grew. Fredi sidled up to her. 'Calm down. I can feel the stress coming off you in waves.'

'You can?' Bonni did her best to regain her composure. Stepping forward, she didn't even hesitate when Quinn opened his arms for a hug.

'Hey, beautiful.' He kept his arm around her when he turned to the women. 'Nice to see you ladies again. This is –' he hooked a thumb at the man next to him – 'my brother, Landon.'

'Ladies.' Landon stepped forward and gave them all kisses on the cheek, which, Bonni could see, went over quite well. There certainly was a drop-dead-gorgeous gene in the Bryant family. The girls were eyeing him like he was a Viking god.

'Where were you last night?' Bonni was a little surprised at Ava's blunt question. Usually, that was Celia's department.

'I got in this morning, before Quinn's tournament.'

'And he won today.' Bonni glanced at Quinn and smiled. She was doing her best to conceal her misgivings about him being a poker player.

'Wow, I'm impressed,' Fredi said. She turned to Landon. 'Do you play?'

He shook his head. 'Nope, the only gambling I do is with the stock market.'

Celia scoffed, and Landon turned to her. She'd remained rather silent through the whole exchange. 'You must be the quiet one?'

'Hardly.'

Landon smiled at her, and Celia looked up at him, her long hair falling down her back. It was like something just zinged between them. Bonni watched with curiosity.

'So nice to meet you.' Her vulnerability from earlier now hidden away, Celia was ready to eat him up.

'Are you having a good time?' Landon stepped toward her and Bonni noticed that Celia seemed to lean in a little closer to Landon. *Yes, this was very interesting indeed.*

'How can you not have a good time in Vegas? As long as none of us ends up in jail or married, we're good.'

Landon laughed. 'And I wonder how many times that's actually happened.'

'Probably far more than we could ever count.'

'I'm sure there's been a lot of quickie divorces. Maybe that's why it's so easy to get a divorce in Nevada. Marriage is for suckers, anyway.'

Bonni looked over at Ava and Fredi and raised her eyebrows. They both nodded and leaned into each other, whispering, before laughing.

Bonni watched them and figured they were talking about Celia. She glanced over to see that Celia and Landon were chatting away.

Quinn tipped his head down to her. 'I wonder what that means?'

'I don't know. But Celia's a handful,' Bonni warned.

'Landon can hold his own,' Quinn assured her.

'I guess we'll see, won't we?'

Landon turned around. 'I know these two have something

up their sleeve, but what about you ladies? Any plans for the rest of the evening?'

'Not really. Maybe play some slots, grab a couple of drinks.' Celia answered for them and shimmied a little closer to him.

Landon looked at his watch. 'Well, I have a little bit of time, before I have to go up for a conference call.'

'At this time of night?' Celia asked.

'Yes, it's not night on the other side of the world.' He gave Celia a rather cute smirk which made her shuffle her feet a little bit.

'Well, then,' Ava interrupted. 'Since you're on borrowed time, how about we get those drinks?'

'An excellent idea,' Landon agreed.

'Right, then, since you guys have yourselves all sorted, I think Bonni and I will move on.' Quinn took her hand.

'Aww, you guys are so cute.' Celia lifted her purse and opened it. 'Do you need any more—'

'Okay, catch you all later.' Bonni wouldn't put it past Celia pull out a handful of condoms in the middle of the bar.

'Time to escape.' Bonni leaned closer to Quinn and whispered, 'Quickly.'

A smile curved his lips. He chuckled, and she figured he understood her haste to leave. She'd deal with the condom situation later.

'We're off.' Quinn wasted no time in leading her out of the bar. He put his arm around her shoulders. 'Now I've got you all to myself.'

'Finally. What do you have in mind?' Bonni snuggled in to him and slipped her arm around his waist.

'Did you eat?' Quinn asked.

Bonni nodded. 'We ate before the show. But if you didn't eat, I'm happy to keep you company.'

He stopped and turned her to face him. Bonni looked up into his deep blue eyes. His touch, look and presence certainly did a number on her. She held her breath, waiting.

'Or we could get room service,' he said, in a low, husky tone.

Bonni's heart beat double time at all the possibilities that could lead to. She didn't have to give it any consideration at all. 'I like it.'

'Good. I think it's an excellent idea too.' Quinn reached for her hand and laced his fingers with hers, gently tugging her closer. 'Shall we?'

Bonni nodded, ready for whatever the night would bring.

Chapter 14

At the risk of sounding like a creeper, there was no way Quinn was letting Bonni leave tonight. Now that he had her safely ensconced in his room, he was determined she would stay until morning. Last night had been all about passion and sex. Tonight, it would be about getting to know her better.

He was captivated by her, watching her, so stunning, as she sat quietly, leaning forward with her elbows on her knees and her chin in her hand, looking out the window.

He thought she was the most serenely beautiful woman he'd ever been with. For a guy in his early thirties, he'd definitely been around. He'd deftly avoid the gold-diggers and the poker bunnies, while enjoying his share of women looking for vacation flings. Quinn had never felt his lifestyle would lend itself to a long-term relationship. But here, after all that, was a woman sitting in his room with a calm presence that soothed his soul. He drew in a deep breath. Since she met him, she had filled an empty hole that seemed so much more significant than it ever had before. Before, he'd filled that hole with his wild life, always looking, seeking, rebelling . . . running, to find whatever it was that was missing in his world.

And now he suspected he'd found it.

'Shall we order?'

'Yes, sounds like a good idea. Whatever you want.' She looked up at him, and he couldn't resist swooping in for a kiss. Her lips softened under his and parted slightly. Quinn reached out with his tongue and swept it along her lips, and she opened them for him. He tasted her and cradled the back of her head, his hand sliding up into her silky hair. When she sighed, he slanted his lips a little more firmly and then reluctantly lifted them from her. She kept her eyes closed and he wanted to think she was savoring the moment as he savored it, by watching a satisfied expression play across her features.

The dark fan of her eyelashes fluttered and then opened. He drew in a breath at the simmering look in her eyes. The lights and evening dusk gave them a smoky-grey appearance, one of mystery and intrigue. He realized he'd yet to see them in the light of day, something he decided then and there to rectify before her vacation ended. And that was a thought he most definitely didn't want even to entertain.

'You're the best kisser,' she told him.

'I'm glad you approve, madam.' Quinn felt his chest puff a little at the compliment.

'Wholeheartedly.'

'Coming from someone as talented in the kissing department as you, that's a high compliment indeed.'

Quinn ran a finger down her cheek before leaning over to grab the room phone. He called down and ordered champagne, sparkling water, chocolate-covered strawberries and an assortment of pastries. When she'd taken her first bite of a croissant earlier that afternoon, she'd made the most delightful moan and he wanted to hear her make it again. He was going to romance her so she'd remember this night for the rest of her life.

He already knew he'd remember it for the rest of his.

'There's a balcony. Would you like to go outside?'

'Absolutely.' Bonni took the hand he held out and he gently pulled her to her feet.

He liked how her hand felt in his and tightened his fingers around hers before letting go and placing it at the curve of her waist. It seemed perfectly natural to guide her. He'd take any excuse to be able to connect and touch her.

'Oh, my. You weren't kidding about the view. It's fantastic.' She walked to the edge of the balcony. 'Look, the mountains. And there's snow on them! Somehow, I hadn't expected that.'

'Is this your first trip to Vegas?' Quinn stepped behind her to wrap her in his arms and she curled into him.

'I've been here once before, but it was a short trip. Didn't have time to do the tourist thing.' She glanced at him with a smile and his chest tightened.

'You weren't in town to have a quickie wedding, were you?' Quinn forced a laugh, but he was tense as he waited for her answer.

'Ha, no, I'm not married. Or dating anyone. Seriously, I mean. With a clean bill of health. For, y'know. Ah, what about you?'

Quinn relaxed and nuzzled her neck. 'Single as single can be. And also healthy. I've got the lowest cholesterol in the family.'

She reached up to lightly swat the back of his head and he grinned down at her. They stood together, quietly, in the crisp air, before Quinn spoke again. 'When are you leaving?'

'Late Monday afternoon. I took vacation days to make it a four-day weekend.' She didn't look happy about it.

It wasn't enough time, especially with him being tied up in

the tournament. 'There's another qualifying round tomorrow morning and then the elimination rounds start in the afternoon. Final rounds are on Monday.'

'Shit. So, you'll be fairly busy for a good portion of the next couple days.'

It wasn't a question, and he felt the restriction of time tighten.

'Yeah.'

'Then we'll have to make the most of tonight and hope for some time together tomorrow.' She looked up at him, and he could tell she was upset. He was glad to see she didn't like the thought of their time together ending either.

He pulled her into his arms. 'Yes. We will.' She shivered. 'Cold?'

'A little.'

'Let's go back inside then.' Quinn wrapped his arm around her shoulder and liked how she snuggled in to him.

'You're so warm.' Bonni hugged him.

'There was a wind out there. It's still early in the year for hot nights.' Quinn never felt the need to pay top dollar for a hotel room in Vegas because he spent so little time in it. Still, he liked to be comfortable, so in addition to the king-sized bed dominating the room, there was a small seating area next to a long ledge that doubled as a desk. He guided Bonni to the small loveseat and they sat, Quinn stretching his legs out in front of them.

'The view was fantastic, though.' Bonni lifted her hands, as if looking for something to fiddle with before folding them together in her lap. 'So where do you call home?'

'Well, a little bit of everywhere, I guess.' Quinn imagined she was trying to start with a softball question, but things were always complicated when it came to his family.

'That's an odd thing to say. How can you be from a little bit of everywhere?'

'Well, we're based on the East Coast, but my family has homes and business interests in numerous places. We did a lot of traveling around.'

Bonni reached out for his hand and he knew she was trying to comfort him. 'Sounds like you had a nomadic upbringing.'

'I guess you could call it that.' He'd already said more than he normally would. Bonni didn't ask any follow-up questions and he was relieved, because explaining about his family was the last thing he wanted to do right now. 'How about you?'

Bonni began idly playing with his fingers. She was one of those people who were always in motion, never content to just sit still. 'Toronto, actually.'

He looked at her with surprise. 'You're Canadian?'

'No,' she laughed, and continued, 'I'm an American citizen, but my father was military. We stayed the longest in Toronto, before he retired to Virginia. I got my criminal psychology degree in college there – that's where I met Ava, Fredi and Celia – and then took some police foundations in Ontario before moving back to Toronto.'

'You have a criminal psychology degree? That . . . that suits you,' he decided. Quinn had noticed how she was always alert in a crowd, not to mention the way she looked after her friends.

Bonni laughed. 'Yeah, I guess being an army brat kept me in that mindset. But I didn't want to enlist, though, because traipsing all over the world was rather hard on a young kid. You've just made friends and then you move on.'

'Wow, I'm impressed. You get more and more interesting every time I talk to you. Do you enjoy life in Canada?'

'Well, I've gotten used to the cold. In fact, I've taken up

skiing and a lot of winter sports. But I much prefer tropical climates, heat. I will probably be moving back to Virginia soon.'

'Why? What do you do for a living?' he asked, highly curious now. Quinn half expected her to say she was FBI.

Bonni dropped his hand and stretched a little, avoiding Quinn's gaze. He couldn't help but notice the way the movement caused her breasts to lift. After another moment of silence, she reluctantly said, 'I work with the cops.'

'Like, as a crime analyst, or a forensic scientist . . .' He could sense this wasn't something she really wanted to talk about. Yet she had. That was huge.

'No. I am a cop. A detective, actually,' she replied. Bonni still wasn't looking at him, so he reached out for a lock of her hair, tangling it around his finger until he saw her watching him out of the corner of her eye.

'You're a cop,' he said, 'I guess I'm rather lucky you didn't clock me one when I grabbed you earlier today.'

He saw her smile, and then she turned to face him again. 'Really lucky. I would've sent you flying. You don't creep up on cops. Or women.'

Quinn wasn't ready for their intimate conversation to turn sensual, but he had to ask. 'Did you bring your handcuffs?'

Bonni rolled her eyes but got off the loveseat, crossing to where she had left her purse. He watched her hips sway, thinking she walked nothing like a cop should walk. Suddenly, taking things slowly tonight seemed like the worst idea ever. She brought her purse back to the loveseat and fished out the thick black wallet he'd seen this morning. 'Nope, just this.'

Quinn took it from her and flipped it open. 'Your badge.' One side had a photo ID card and a metal badge was on the other. He ran his fingers over the badge before closing and handing it back.

'So, Detective Connolly, what department are you in?'

'Fraud. It's mostly white-collar stuff, money-laundering, and some gaming stuff.' And she gave him a stare that made him understand why she had been reluctant to tell him she was a cop.

Bonni held her breath as she waited for Quinn's response. If he was mixed up in something shady, this could be the end of everything right now. Instead, he reached down and grabbed her legs, swinging them on to his lap. He grunted a little when her boots accidentally dug into his finely toned stomach. 'No worries, Detective, I only play in sanctioned events or for recreational purposes. Doing illegal shit is a good way to stop getting invited to the big-ticket events.'

It was a good answer, but not enough information for Bonni. 'How did you become a professional gambler?'

'Not sure, really. I've been gambling in some capacity or another for as long as I can remember.' Quinn undid her laces on and slipped her boots off her feet.

Bonni sensed he was being cautious with his replies. He began to massage her feet again, but she didn't let the intense pleasure distract her. 'Even when you were a kid? You gambled then?'

'You know what it's like getting shuffled from place to place as a kid. Even in the States, there's always a different culture, different rules and traditions to learn. But making bets, playing poker – some things are universal. But in fact it started with horse racing.'

She tried to analyze his facial expression, but he seemed focused on her feet, his hands starting to move up her calves. Quinn had the epitome of a poker face. 'Horse racing?'

'Yes, I was around racehorses most of my life. My dad owned a number of them. It was only natural I'd start reading the *Racing Form* and learning how to handicap.'

'A natural progression, I guess.' Quinn had been right. It had sucked, constantly moving. Still, there were usually other kids on the bases, other kids who knew what it was like to be afraid of a parent getting deployed, of having their lives shuffled around at the directive of some anonymous paper-pusher. She would just wander around until she came across a pick-up basketball game or a skateboard half-pipe. Quinn, though . . . She could tell that Quinn and Landon had come from money. They'd mentioned their mother in passing a few times, but never their father. But gambling? For his entire life? To the point that he made a career of it? It was a giant red flag for her.

'Well, to each their own. Everyone has their own coping methods, I suppose.' Bonni cringed inside, realizing that she sounded judgmental, exactly what she'd been trying to avoid.

Quinn turned toward her, and she saw concern in his eyes. She didn't know what to say to change the course of the conversation and stop it from going down a path that would likely ruin their evening. That's the last thing she wanted to do. But there was nothing he could say that would make her feel better right now, so she seized on the first topic that came to mind.

'What time do you have to be there tomorrow?' she asked.

'The first game is at nine, but I have to leave at about eight in order to get everything sorted.' He stopped rubbing her legs and instead held them in a firm grip.

'Maybe I should go back down and stay with the girls for the night then,' she suggested.

He reached for her waist, pulling her forward until she was forced to straddle him or risk falling off the loveseat. 'Absolutely not. I want you here with me. There's no need to feel like you should leave.' The look in his eyes brooked no argument.

'You're sure? I do have my own room, you know. And it's quite a lovely one, at that. If you need to be rested for the morning, I totally understand.' Bonni wasn't sure whether she wanted Quinn to let her go so that she could have a reprieve to sort out her feelings or if she wanted him to continue to demand that she stay.

'You're welcome to leave anytime – I'd never force you to stay – but don't ever think I'm kicking you out or asking you to leave.'

'Okay, then. Understood.' She was glad the conversation had veered slightly. He pressed his lips together and nodded. There was a new tightness at the edge of his mouth and it saddened her to know that she had put it there.

She tried again to read the expression on his features. Was he hiding things now? She hoped not, but then, in reality, everyone had something to hide. Everyone chose their path in life and had to live with the outcomes. Bonni shifted. She could feel his muscular thighs below her. It reminded her that this was supposed to be a vacation fling. She started to lean forward to kiss him, but he pulled back a little, saying, 'Bonni, I think—'

A knock at the door broke the heaviness of the moment.

'Saved by the proverbial bell.' Bonni slid off him, and he stood. She watched him walk to the door. She liked him. A lot. Was it realistic to think past Vegas? She shook her head slightly. No, it wasn't. Like any vacation fling, it ended with them going their separate ways and carrying on with their lives. But, wow, did that make her heart hurt. She glanced at the door and watched the exchange between Quinn and the room-service waiter. Did his career choice really matter anyway when, realistically, there was no future for them?

'Nope.' The server pushed a large table containing covered silver platters and champagne chilling in an ice bucket into the room. She stood to investigate the platters while Quinn dealt with signing the charge slip and the tip. As he closed the door behind the room-service waiter, she said, 'How lovely. Look at the white linen, and the way the silver and the crystal sparkle in the light.'

'Only the best for you.' He placed a kiss on her cheek and a shiver of delight rippled through her. Bonni slid her arms around his waist and was relieved when he hugged her shoulder. Maybe everything would be okay.

He reached out to lift the champagne from the ice bucket. 'Feel like a glass?'

Bonni had to laugh. 'This seems to be a champagne trip.'

Quinn released her to pop the champagne and she took a step or two back. Without a word, he took the bottle from the bucket, expertly removed the wire cage and foil wrapper, took a towel and twisted the cork. The result was a muffled pop. He didn't spill a drop.

'That was a very civilized way to open a bottle of champagne. Most people have corks flying and champagne everywhere.'

Quinn poured the bubbling liquid into their glasses. 'It's the best way to open a bottle and not waste any.'

'I don't know much about champagne. And I haven't really had a lot of it until this trip.'

Bonni took the flute he handed her and they clinked glasses before she took a sip. The fizzy taste danced on her tongue. 'Fredi isn't a fan of champagne, but the others love it. I'm good either way. Although this is absolutely wonderful.'

'It should be. It's Cristal. Where else can you treat yourself but on vacation?'

'That wasn't the original plan, but I won a jackpot on the slots yesterday. Champagne has been flowing ever since.'

'You won the slots? I love to hear about people winning against the house. Nothing like winning and taking home casino money.' Quinn toasted her with his glass.

'Yes, just after we arrived. I know I should do something

practical with my unexpected windfall, but I won it on the complimentary voucher they gave us for booking our rooms. I feel like it's free all the way around, so why not make it an extra-special trip for my friends?' She took another sip, suddenly feeling as light and bubbly as the champagne. She turned to look up at him and he swooped down, capturing her mouth in a brief, promising kiss.

'You have such an amazingly generous heart. Not many people would share the wealth like that.' Quinn's voice deepened, and Bonni's airy feeling popped as a thread of warmth snaked through her.

'Maybe you're just hanging out with the wrong people.' She gave him a questioning look.

'Or maybe I've just found the right one.' A delicious tremor ran through her at the seductive look and subtle message he gave her.

Feeling flirtatious, she bent over a little more than necessary to lift the cover off the first platter. 'Oooh, pastries. Your sweet tooth at work again, Quinn?'

Bonni looked up to find his gaze fixed on her cleavage. He lifted his eyes to meet hers and she felt a little breathless.

'Oh, I think you know, Temptress, what I'm hungry for. Some of the greatest pleasures in life are good food and good sex—'

'Great sex,' she interjected.

He winked at her and replied. 'Yes, *great* sex.' Bonni shivered with delight at the warmth that grew between her thighs. 'Also, excellent wine, good friends and the company of a beautiful woman.'

Bonni looked into his eyes. The banter faded away and it was just the two of them sitting across the table, with the candlelight and the glow from the Vegas strip reflecting into the room.

'I'm really glad you're here, with me.' Quinn's voice was low, and the deep intimacy of the tone, reverberated inside her. He took her hand and she turned hers over, curling her fingers around his.

'Me too. I don't normally do things like this, so it certainly was a surprise meeting you and ending up here with you.' She was astounded how easy it was to tell him things. Well, maybe not all things, but some things.

He nodded, and didn't let go of her hand, using his other to refill their glasses.

'Yes, it is a surprise. The best one of my life.'

Chapter 15

Hearing Quinn's amazingly romantic words, Bonni wasn't sure whether to strip off her clothes and tackle him or run screaming from the inevitable heartbreak that seemed to be looming before her. Luckily, she heard her phone chime in her bag and peeled herself away to check it.

Ava xo: *I hope you are having a good time with Q! Don't worry about us, I'm keeping an eye on Celia and Fredi. They are currently dirty dancing with Landon.*

Bonni: *Thought he had a call?*

Ava xo: *Ya, over now. He invited us to another dance club and everyone's treating him like he is a sheikh or something, with us as his harem lol!*

Bonni laughed and showed the message to Quinn. He shook his head and chuckled.

'That's Landon for you. They're in for a load of fun trouble if they're out with him.'

'My girls can handle it. I want them to have a good time.'

'Because if they're having a good time, it makes you feel better about being here with me and not them?'

Bonni met his gaze. 'You're very perceptive. And, yes, it eases my mind. Is he married? Or in a relationship with anybody?' Bonni needed to ask, always feeling the need to protect her friends.

'Now, no. He hasn't been in a serious relationship for a while. His business takes him away a lot. Some women have a hard time with that.'

'I have to admit, I'm not sure I blame them. No girl likes to be second best. What does he do?'

Quinn finished the champagne and put the glass down. 'I think we've talked enough about other people for now. Let's turn off our phones and just focus on us. How about some music?'

'An excellent idea.' He took her phone from her and she watched him put it on 'do not disturb'. Then he scrolled through his phone before finding the song he wanted and tapped Play before placing it on the desk.

'Sexual Healing' by Marvin Gaye came on. Bonni turned to face Quinn and draped her arms over his shoulder. He looked down into her eyes and it astounded her once more that a simple look from him could ignite her so quickly. She walked her fingers up his neck and pressed the back of his head so he'd bend down toward her.

'I've been waiting for a kiss all night. Maybe we can do some of our own sexual healing?'

'You don't have to ask me twice.'

Quinn swept her up into his arms and she wrapped her legs around his hips. He held her with ease and fastened his mouth to hers. She breathed him in, loving the way his essence filled her, the firm yet gentle way his hands gripped her bottom, the heat of his body next to her core.

She wanted this man with every fiber of her being.

He carried her to the loveseat in front of the window. He slid his hands to her hips and allowed her to slip down his body until her toes touched the floor, all the while never lifting his mouth from hers.

Could he feel her heart? It pounded painfully in her chest, pumping her heavy and languid blood through her veins. She clutched him a little tighter as she tottered, her legs feeling rubbery.

He pulled back from her. 'Still in?'

'Yes, all in, so very all in. You have a way with me.'

He smiled and tilted his head sideways. 'That's what I like to hear.'

Bonni pulled at his shirt and had it off, tossing it to the floor, and he quickly undid his pants.

Quinn had her clothes off in no time.

'Quinn, won't people see us?'

She looked out the window and he pulled her so her back was flush to his chest. Bonni pushed her bottom into him and shivered at the insistent press of his cock behind her, the heat from his chest.

'So what if they do?' He shuffled her forward until she was right in front of the window.

'Quinn.' Bonni placed her palms on the glass.

'Be brave, my lady cop . . . be daring. You might like the thrill.'

He gently pushed her closer to the glass, and Bonni looked down. They were high. She could see people on the streets, the streetlights dispelling the night shadows. If they looked up, would they see her? The windows in the hotel across from theirs could easily be seen. She knew she could be too. He was right, it was thrilling. Daring.

'A little closer,' he urged.

'The glass is cold,' Bonni whispered, but she let him move her until her nipples touched it. She gasped at the chill as her sensitive flesh pebbled at the shock. But God, it was a turn-on. Bonni, rotated her hips without really knowing she was doing it and Quinn groaned behind her.

'Ah, woman, you are a constant surprise to me.' He reached around, taking hold of her breast, and Bonni pressed into the warmth of his hand, her nipple deliciously pressing into his palm.

He slid his fingers over her belly, then lower, and she sagged against him when he pressed into her folds and found her clitoris.

'Quinn, n-not here.' She moaned.

'Yes, here.'

Her head fell back on his shoulders and she reached back, grabbing his ass. Doing that arched her back even more, giving him all the easy access to her breasts and pussy he wanted.

His cock pressed between her ass cheeks and she pulsed her hips until he groaned. His fingers increased their demand on her and she clung to him. Here. Before the floor-to-ceiling windows, exposed to anyone that looked up. Bonni didn't give a damn anymore.

'O–oh, Quinn.' She gasped as her release began to tighten in her belly. She increased the tempo of her hips and it enhanced the sensations of his fingers.

'Come for me, Bonni. Here, at the window, for the world to see, to know that you're mine.'

And she did. Her body shuddered in his arms and her legs buckled. Quinn held her tight, as she knew he would.

'Oh my God.' Bonni was weak as a newborn kitten, and as Quinn swept her into his arms, she put hers around his neck and he carried her to the couch. She looked up at him. 'Please tell me you have condoms.'

'I'll be right back.'

Bonni lay on the couch, the slightly rough material rubbing against her sensitive skin. Quinn returned, still hard. She reached up and grasped him, slowly stroking his length. He held up a condom.

'You left some behind.' He ripped it open and sheathed himself.

'Damn good thing my friends were well stocked.'

'Yes, a damn good thing.'

Bonni spread her legs and reached for him. Quinn kneeled between her thighs.

'I'm so ready for you, Quinn.' Bonni was almost panting.

She reached between them and guided him in to her.

He thrust deep and slow, drawing out their pleasure. Bonni held him in the cradle of her thighs as he steadied into a cadence that had her soaring back up to the heights of desire.

'Now, Quinn, I want you to come for me.' Bonni whispered into his ear as he enveloped her in his arms, holding her so tightly she could barely catch her breath.

She turned his face to her, wanting to see him. His eyes were closed, and the passion etched on his face thrilled her. Bonni licked his lips, his mouth opened for her, and their tongues tangled together. The power built in him, and transferred to her. She tried to hold off her orgasm, waiting for him to come first, but she couldn't.

He ground into her, his roar of release echoed off the walls and they lay spent and breathless, entwined in each other's arms.

*

That had only been the first round. When Bonni woke, hours later, she was delightfully sore. She stretched a little, the bed sheets cool against her bare skin. She was also a little hungry, despite Quinn feeding her strawberries and pastries after a very fun game of Bad Cop, Begging Robber. The room was dark, and Quinn's breathing was deep and steady. She looked at him lying next to her and she knew she was beginning to fall for him. It was more than just sex. The personal information he'd already shared, it made her want to know more about him. To explore all the layers of Quinn, deeply and intimately, to know him and build a future with him outside of the boundaries of a vacation fling, but she had no idea if that was even a possibility.

She caught sight of the alarm clock and realized he'd have to get up very soon for his tournament. His poker tournament. The most recent event in his very long history of gambling. She should go. She didn't want to disturb him and throw off his morning routine again. Bonni began to slowly shift out of the bed, but paused. It was harder than she would've imagined to leave him. It had been such an amazing night, and she wanted more. She wanted to slide down his body, to wake him with her mouth, to have him look at her with his incredible eyes, dimmed by sleep, before he touched her with his agile hands.

But that would be selfish. He needed to focus. And what about her friends? Yes, her friends. She should really check on them, and this vacation was about spending time with them, after all. Half falling for a life-long gambler with no roots had not been part of the plan.

Bonni slid out of bed quietly, grabbed her clothes and went into the bathroom to dress. Silently, she padded back into the bedroom to collect her boots and her purse. Again, she stopped, looking down at Quinn. He had turned on his side, his arm flung out, like he was reaching for her. She fought the urge to climb back into bed, to at least kiss him goodbye. Instead she scribbled him a quick note and left it by the lamp. In less than thirty-six hours, she'd be on a plane, starting her journey back to Toronto. *This isn't one of Ava's movies, Bonni. There's no fairy godmother to magic you up a happy ending.*

She slipped out the door and closed it quietly behind her.

Chapter 16

Bonni tapped her key card and the door unlocked. As quietly as she had left Quinn's room, she slipped into the suite, not wanting to wake up any of her friends. Were they even home yet?

The living room was dark, as were the bedrooms. Soft snoring came from behind the half-closed doors. Her friends must be sleeping off another wild night. Bonni pulled off her boots and held them, tiptoeing across the marble floor. She weaved her way through the furniture in the dark and wished her eyes would adjust more quickly. Tripping over a chair would definitely wake them all up and then cause a whack of interrogation.

'What are you doing here?' a voice greeted her in the dark.

Bonni nearly jumped out of her skin, dropping her boots with a clatter on the floor. 'What the hell, Ava! You nearly gave me a heart attack.' She had to catch her breath.

'Sorry, didn't mean to scare you. Why aren't you with Quinn?' Ava's voice was quiet in the darkened room.

Bonni slid on to the couch beside her. It was comforting to

be sitting on a couch with her friend again. She wiggled a little, folding her legs beneath her. 'Why are you up?'

Even in the shadows, Bonni could see the look Ava shot her. 'Bonni, I can tell you have something on your mind. Stop deflecting.'

Bonni slowly shook her head, not in denial but in confusion. 'You constantly surprise me with your perception.' She flopped back and shifted to put her feet on the coffee table.

She felt Ava's hand on her thigh. 'Come on, Bon, it's okay. Talk to me.'

Bonni sighed and let herself relax into the plush cushions. 'Quinn,' she whispered.

'What about him? Did you finally accept that he's the man of your dreams?'

It was no surprise to Bonni that Ava immediately went to the happily-ever-after place, but it wasn't so simple.

'I really like him, but everything is moving so fast it's scaring me. Plus, I live in Canada, and he has no roots. He basically roams around the globe looking for a good poker game.'

'That doesn't mean he can't put down roots in Canada. Yeah, maybe he'd leave, but he'd always come back to you.' Ava rubbed Bonni's leg reassuringly.

'You think so?' Bonni wanted to believe her friend so badly. 'But maybe, over time, it would feel like a trap.'

'Maybe. Or maybe, over time, it would feel like home. And, remember, you're not staying in Canada for ever. Only another six months or so, isn't it?'

Bonni wasn't sure about what Ava just said. She couldn't decide if the move to Virginia and being more hands-on with her dad would make things better or worse. She stared at her feet, wiggling her toes and lost in thought.

Ava leaned forward to set the thick crystal tumbler Bonni

hadn't known she was holding on to the coffee table and the ice cubes clinked. She liked Scotch on the rocks. Why had Ava been sitting alone in the dark? Before Bonni could ask, Ava spoke, 'Bonni, I need you to hear something.'

'What?' Bonni twisted her torso so that she was facing her friend more fully.

Ava took her hand and squeezed it. Bonni got the impression the physical touch was a connection her friend sorely needed.

'I've never told you this. I haven't told anybody this. Because it's way too painful for me to dredge back up. Because I know now what a huge mistake I made. A mistake made for selfish reasons, reasons that remain unrealized.'

'Ava, what are you saying?'

Her friend took another beat before answering, as if gathering her strength. 'About five years ago, there was a man who was everything I dreamed of. Quinn reminds me of him in certain ways.' She closed her eyes and drew in a deep breath.

Bonni watched the emotions play across her face and knew Ava was recalling bittersweet and painful memories. Bonni had a feeling she wasn't going to like what Ava was about to tell her. Ava opened her eyes and Bonni's heart nearly broke at the despair in them.

'Ava, what? You're scaring me.'

'We met on a business trip. The client was based in Dallas and he was there as a consultant from his firm in London. Our connection was instantaneous. Similar to you and Quinn. Anyway, we didn't fight it and began a passionate, crazy, wonderful fling. We kept it secret, though, as we didn't want our colleagues gossiping about us. I have to admit, the secrecy added a spice to things. The sex was out of this world. But it was more than that, there was something deeper.'

Bonni knew precisely what Ava was referring to. 'That exactly describes me and Quinn.'

Ave fell back on the couch and her voice trembled. 'I know, I can see it.'

'What happened?' Bonni leaned forward and gave Ava's hand a squeeze.

'We couldn't figure out how to make it work. We talked about giving up our respective careers, changing our lives, but neither of us, at the time, was willing to do that.' She shrugged a shoulder. 'So we went our separate ways. We never thought about a long-distance relationship either. It just ended.'

Ava freed her hand from Bonni's grip to press her fingers against her eyes. All this time, one of her best friends had been carrying around this secret heartbreak, the pain too much to speak of, but now she was baring her soul to give a cautionary tale. The love Bonni felt for her friend was overwhelming.

'Oh, Ava, I never knew. You should've talked to me. I could've helped you through it. Have you gotten over him?'

'I don't know really. I think I have. But in a way, it doesn't matter. It's still one of the biggest regrets of my life.' The hurt in her voice was evident, but there was also strength and Bonni drew from it.

Ava shifted to grab her drink off the table and downed the remainder. She waved the empty glass as she continued, 'God, I can't believe how similar it is to you and Quinn! But what's important for me to tell you is this. I'm in my early thirties, I'm settled in a job I mostly love, even if it wasn't my childhood dream. I've tried dating, online and real life, and it's a zoo. I'm so sick of the ghosting, breadcrumbing, and all the other bs that accompany dating. So many frogs, Bonni, and I'm tired of kissing them.'

'Ava – I . . .' Bonni wasn't exactly sure what she was going to say, but this uncharacteristic bitterness was so unlike her friend.

Ava held up her hand. 'No, let me finish. Despite all that, I do want to find someone. Someone that gets me, and thinks I'm amazing, and holy hell! wants to build a life together. So I'm holding on to hope! Even if I'm a silver-haired bride, I will keep looking and not let the right man slip out of my fingers again.'

'Maybe it's not too late, maybe you could track him down – I could help—'

Ava shook her head. 'It was five years ago and I've moved on . . . alone. Besides, I tell myself that if we'd really been meant to be we would have fought for each other. We would have made any sacrifice to be with each other. But like I said, we simply . . . fell apart.'

Bonni had always considered herself a fighter. Some people rolled with the punches and adapted to life, but not Bonni. Whether it was a perceived injustice or simply a goal she had set for herself, she always left the gate swinging. So, was Quinn worth fighting for?

Ava tilted her head sideways. 'Bonni, I'd never tell you what to do, unless you ask me for advice, but I wanted to give you food for thought.' She leaned forward and pulled Bonni into a bear hug. 'We girls have to look out for each other.'

After a long hug they both sorely needed, they stood up. Ava's voice brightened. 'Anyway, I'm on Team Boing—'

'Boing? Do I even want to know?' Bonni braced herself for more of her friends' craziness.

'It's your couple name! Bo for you and In for Quinn, and a G to make it pop. Fredi and Celia came up with it.' Bonni was glad to hear the humor in Ava's tone.

They laughed quietly.

'Remember our junior year, we got that two-bedroom suite and we used to do this in the mornings?' Bonni recalled. 'Celia and Fredi would be passed out from the night before and you and I would go to the common room and eat cereal and talk?'

'Of course I remember. They were some of the best times of my life. I feel so fortunate we've formed these lasting friendships'

'Me too.

Bonni yawned, and Ava did too. Bonni bent over and retrieved her boots from the floor. 'I feel like I've been hit by a truck. Gotta close my eyes for a while.'

'Me too. You know those two will be up early and ready to hit the town.'

'Ugh, I can't even . . . Give me a few hours. Night, hun.'

'Sweet dreams of your hunky man,' Ava whispered, and padded off to her bed.

Bonni stumbled through the darkened room to her bedroom. Removing her clothes, she dropped them on the floor and face-planted into the bed and pillows. She thought for sure she'd be out like a light, but Quinn invaded her mind. And so did Ava's heartbreaking admission.

There was still so much to know about him. The private stuff, like who he was, where he came from, what he did for a living – aside from poker – and where he called home and how, if possible, they could fit it all together. Lying in the dark, her eyes growing heavier, Bonni made a decision that allowed her to begin drifting off to sleep. Her chaotic brain finally shut down.

I have to take a leap of faith. It was unknown territory she'd be jumping into. But something told her she could trust Quinn to catch her.

Chapter 17

Sun streamed through the window and Bonni listened to see if the others were awake. All quiet.

She'd slept for a while but had finally turned on the TV and got sucked into one of her favorite movies: *The Terminator*. She thought one of the most romantic lines ever was when Kyle Reese tells Sarah Connor that he came across time for her.

It made Bonni realize she *did* want that too. She wanted romance, love and devotion. She was antsy and leapt out of bed. After a hot shower and fresh clothes she decided she desperately needed coffee. Checking the time, her belly did a little flip as she thought about Quinn. This time yesterday she had been naked in his bed. Immediately, she replayed their love-making from last night. She shivered, unable to believe she'd been so bold next to the window. It had been amazingly erotic and she found herself growing warm inside at the memory. Quinn was right, after whispering in her ear during one of their private moments, that it was important to create memories. It was something she would take to heart. And the more time she spent thinking of him, the more she believed that she wanted to create memories *with* him.

She wondered what he'd thought when he woke up to find her gone. She hoped he'd found the note so he didn't think she'd taken off on him.

Bonni quietly opened the bedroom door and listened again, before breathing a sigh of relief that she'd be able to get her morning started without being questioned by her friends. But she did make sure there was no one lurking in chairs, ready to scare the shit out of her again.

Quinn would probably already be in his first game. She grabbed her flat white coffee and a biscotti from Starbucks in the lobby. She munched and drank as she swiftly made her way out of the hotel to the Bellagio.

The streets were relatively quiet, with not many people on them this early, and Bonni realized it was the first time she'd actually been outside during the day since they'd arrived in Vegas. She looked at all the buildings, the brand-new hotels, at the conference center. It certainly had changed in ten years.

The pedestrian bridges were saviors. Even if they did add extra steps to your walk, she could imagine the number of people that avoided getting hit by the crazy traffic as they tried to run across the street. Maybe she'd take the elevator instead of the escalator. It was closer. She picked up her pace, wanting to get to the hotel.

In the ballroom, she read the standings by the players' registration and information area. Bonni couldn't believe what she was seeing. She saw Quinn's name, and he was in the top three. Her jaw fell open at the winnings listed beside the players' names. Bonni's eyes nearly popped out of her head. Quinn was cleaning up.

She wandered around, keeping to the back of room and

skirting the tables and crowds, watching from a distance. The tables were broken up into areas behind hip-high divider curtains. She stopped close to one table and watched the game. She'd seen a sign earlier that it was a Texas Hold 'Em tournament.

She scanned the crowd for Quinn. He wouldn't be easy to spot, that was for sure. A lot of the players seemed to have a certain way of dressing: hoodies with baseball caps and sunglasses. She'd chased more hoodie wearers than she cared to remember, but these people likely had more money than she could shake a stick at.

Bonni milled around a bit more, pondering the difference between drug dealers and embezzlers. White-collar criminals steal from pensions, siphon off savings, ruin people's livelihood, while drug cartels peddle their products for millions of dollars and start people down paths that could destroy their lives. But at least drug addicts knew what they were getting into. White-collar victims were merely sacrificial lambs, at the mercy of the wealthy who wanted to get wealthier. Where did professional gamblers fall on the spectrum? An addiction to gambling could be as damaging as an addiction to drugs, and these players willingly signed up to potentially lose money. All for the slim chance of being a big winner. She drew in a deep sigh and tried not to let herself be mind-boggled about the decisions people made. She found a seat in the shadow of a pillar. Perfect.

She sat and wished she had her own baseball cap to hide beneath. She watched the tables in front of her. At this one, to her untrained eye, it looked like there was a ton of money in chips floating around. She carefully inspected each player's face, except the two of them who had their backs to her. Bonni decided she'd stay for a few more minutes and then move on to another table. She hadn't thought to look and see if there was a seating chart. Then one of the players moved in a way that made her heart jump. The dude wore a purple LA Kings cap and had made a movement that reminded her of Quinn.

He tilted his head and stretched his shoulders. Something that Quinn did. Now all her focus was on him. She looked at the monitors – many were placed around the room, offering a better viewing angle of the players – waiting for a clear camera angle so she could see his face and double-check that she was right. It took about five minutes before the camera got him, and it was because he had won the hand. He raked in about $275,000. Bonni nearly choked on her now cold flat white.

'Excuse me, is that typical winnings?' she asked the older gentleman sitting next to her. He seemed very intent on watching the players and she hoped he didn't mind her interruption.

'This was a rich pot. And they're only going to get higher from here. My money is on the guy in the purple hat to win.'

Bonni felt a surge of emotion for Quinn, and it shocked the shit out of her. The man was talking about Quinn. Her Quinn . . . well, not technically, but suddenly the thought of him being *her Quinn* was what she wanted. 'That guy with our back to us? You think he's going to win?'

'Unless he royally screws up. He's dominating that table, and so he's a lock to advance to the next round.'

Bonni watched the table and then turned to the man. He was still watching the game. 'I don't know much about this tournament. Or poker, for that matter.'

He glanced at her and smiled. 'Well, don't be too hard on yourself. A lot of people here have no clue what it's all about. They just like to watch. The money intrigues them.'

'I imagine it would. Have you been in a tournament before?'

'No, no. I'm not good enough, plus, my wife would kill me. We just happened to be here at the same time as this tournament. I like to watch them on television.'

'Thanks for the info.' Bonni crossed her legs and rested her arms on her knee. She was fascinated by this whole thing. Especially after her neighbor started explaining what was happening. She sensed he was quite focused on what was going on, and it made her wonder if you could bet on the outcome. Anything was possible in Vegas.

It was about an hour later and the final hand was played. Quinn won.

'See? I told you he would if he didn't screw something up.' The man gathered up his things and stood. 'He's got a talent, that man.' He checked his watch. 'Perfect timing too. My wife's spa treatment will be just about finished and she won't even know I was here. You keep your eye on him. He'll go far.' The man pointed at Quinn.

Bonni smiled at him. 'Thanks again for explaining everything. You were very helpful. And I *will* keep an eye on that player.' If only he knew just how close an eye she'd be keeping on Quinn.

The people at the table stood to do a round of hand-shaking and Bonni held her breath. She was on eggshells, waiting for Quinn to turn and see her in the crowd. She wanted to stay and wait for him, and knew her friends would be preoccupied with their own stuff. They had texted her when they finally woke up. Celia said she had some writing to do, while Fredi and Ava had decided to go to the hot tub and pool. Bonni knew she had some time.

He stretched his back and turned around. Bonni watched him, realizing Ava was right. She was breathless around Quinn. He certainly was magnificent looking. But under his perfection was a passionate and sensitive and, *oh yes*, a demanding man who had made love to her all night long, two nights in a row. A man that brought her to heights of pleasure she'd never before experienced. But he was also a man who was more than just a lover and a poker player. He was a man that had sparked a curiosity in her that was becoming all-consuming.

And she wanted more of him. The thought of them going their separate ways at the end of their Vegas trip pained her. That in itself was a huge admission. She couldn't refute their swift, tumultuous and indescribable connection.

He searched the audience as if he were looking for someone, and she got a thrill of pleasure thinking that he might be looking for her. Or perhaps he was looking for Landon? Of course, she hadn't thought about him. She didn't like that as much. Bonni stayed where she was and continued to watch, leaning forward to look around the pillar. If Landon was here, then she would slip quietly away without any fuss. No point in creating a hullabaloo by being present when she wasn't expected. The crush of people didn't allow her to see anything beyond the immediate area, so she stood up to look back at Quinn's table and discovered he'd found her in the crowd. He had a big smile on his face. Bonni's heart jumped, and she returned his smile, feeling it stretch her cheeks wide. It was involuntary. She wouldn't have been able to control it if she had tried. Since meeting Quinn, she'd turned into a grinning fool and, as she wove her way through the seats toward him, Bonni accepted that she didn't mind the least little bit.

'I wasn't expecting to see you here.' Quinn reached over and grasped her shoulders, drawing her in for a kiss. 'Could you be my lucky charm?'

She loved that he didn't have a fear of PDA, kissing her in the midst of all the people here, at a poker tournament with television cameras everywhere. It gave her another insight into his character. He was his own man.

Bonni pointed at the table. 'I don't think you need any kind of luck. That's quite a haul.'

'Hm, oh, yes, it was a strong table, but I'm looking forward to tomorrow. That's where the real competition lies. How long have you been here?'

'A little while.' A seed of unease planted itself in her belly at how cavalierly he treated the money.

'Come.' He took her hand and they walked side by side, the divider curtain between them, until they rounded to the entryway.

'So what did you think?' he asked her.

'I don't know how you do it. It takes a lot of guts to play cards like that. And the money, I simply can't get over the money.' She shook her head in wonder.

Bonni briefly thought about texting her partner to ask him to do a background check on Quinn, but she wouldn't, fully aware of the can of worms she could be opening. It was unethical, since he was not under any kind of investigation, and, really, it was none of her business where he got the money. At least at this point in their blossoming ... what? Relationship? If they were going to have a shot at making this work, she had to trust him, not snoop around in his world. If she went behind his back, it wouldn't be something she could ever come back from. She had to trust that he would open up to her when the time was right.

Although time was something they were running out of.

'You get used to it. Winning keeps me in the game. Building points makes sponsors happy and means I get to keep moving on. It's fluid, and I'm always ready to go where the game is.'

Okay, so he sorta told me. He plays off his winnings. She bit her lip, as the seed of unease just sprouted a little stem. Would he ever be able to put down roots or would he continue to travel around the world, always chasing the next game?

They had to sidestep around a crowd of people, so separated, but came back together.

'Have you had breakfast or anything to eat?' Bonni asked him.

'Yes, I had something earlier. I'm going to be tied up here pretty much most of the day.' He looked at his watch. 'But I do have a bit of time before they call for the next round.'

'I have no idea how you can just keep going from one to the next.'

'This one is organized a little differently. It's over just three days, and it's an invitational tournament. Most tournaments run for a week.'

'So for an invitational tournament, you have to be really good, eh?'

He looked down at her. 'Yes.' There was a thrill shining in his eyes, driven by something that was so far from her wheelhouse she wondered if she'd ever be able to understand. 'Have you eaten?' Quinn asked.

She shrugged her shoulders. 'I had a coffee and a biscotti on the walk over.'

'Well, I could use a coffee. Let's go grab one over there.' He took her hand, and he kept her close this time when they had to dodge between people lingering around the ring of tables near the refreshment station. 'Landon texted me – he's nursing quite a hangover. Apparently, Celia drank him under the table.'

Bonni laughed. 'I told you he'd have his hands full. Celia can pack 'em back for a little thing.'

Quinn chuckled, and Bonni shivered with delight when he put his hand on her waist.

'Let's sit over there.' Quinn slid his hand up her back, his fingers strong and totally reminding her of their magic touch. He guided her to a small table in a bustling café. His presence had a powerful effect on her. She absorbed the sensations he roused in her, the thrill of his touch and the delightful seductive quiver that flowed through her body. The sense of security she had around him . . . and . . . something else had her in a state. She eyed him, watching how he fussed with the chair, before motioning for her to sit, and realized it was his attention to her. *He cared?* Bonni smiled to herself and was glad she'd come to the tournament now. She'd never really been treated like a lady before. Her line of work made it hard to be feminine; she'd always been just one of the guys, both at work and growing up. Bonni had figured the girlie gene had never made its way into her DNA. Yet, here, in the presence of this man, she was feeling everything womanly.

And she liked it.

'I was surprised you were gone this morning. I didn't hear you leave.'

She gazed at him and saw that he wasn't accusing her, he wasn't judging, yet the look in his eyes was something she hadn't seen before. Soft, calm and with an almost-yearning in them. The layers were peeling back and Bonni tried to see deeper. *Just what did the expression in his gaze mean?*

She cleared her throat, suddenly thrown off kilter. 'I tried to be quiet so I didn't wake you. I don't sleep well. When I wake up, it's hard to get back to sleep. Plus, I knew you had to be up early today for this tournament. I didn't want to be an unnecessary distraction for you.'

She dropped her gaze and caught her breath, trying to steady her pounding heart. Something that had become oh so common since meeting Quinn.

He put his finger under her chin to tilt her face up, smiled and leaned forward. 'That was thoughtful of you. But I missed you in my bed.'

Bonni drew in a quick breath; his voice was low, deep and seductive, just loud enough for her to hear. Memories of their shared intimacy reignited her desire for him. He pressed a kiss to her lips, light, sensual, so when he did lift up from her, she sat for a moment with her eyes closed, craving more and totally forgetting they were in the middle of a busy café.

Bonni blinked and focused on him. 'You are a dangerous man, Quinn Bryant.' She raised the coffee cup and gulped a mouthful, then lowered it, still holding it between her hands.

'Dangerous in a good way, I hope.'

She nodded and met his gaze. 'Yes, in a very good way.' A blush rushed up her cheeks, and it surprised her.

Quinn laughed and placed his hand over hers. 'I like that you can still blush.'

She shook her head and raised her eyebrows. 'I can't believe I still have the ability. Honestly, it's annoying.'

'No, it's not annoying, it's nice.' Quinn caught her gaze and Bonni fell under his spell. 'I know what you look like when you fly to pieces.'

Bonni looked around quickly. 'Quinn, we're in public, you can't say that here.' But she wanted him to continue. This dirty talk wasn't what she was used to, and she liked the excitement of it.

Quinn leaned back in the chair, which was really too small for his large frame, and his chest expanded as he drew in a deep breath. 'Why are you worried someone will hear?' He gave her a slow smile, which was her undoing. 'So, let them be jealous. You're mine.'

She drew in a gasp and closed her eyes, savoring his words.

He reached for her hand and took it in his. 'You need to stay in bed with me, then you'll sleep well.'

'You might be too much of a distraction for me to be able to sleep.' Bonni lifted a shoulder and gave him a coquettish smile.

'I'm quite happy to be your favorite distraction. And your wildest fantasy.' He lowered his head so that he was gazing at her from beneath his eyebrows. Bonni giggled.

'Perhaps I need to know some of your fantasies.' Bonni tipped her head to the side, waiting to see what his response would be.

'And that, my sexy detective, is just fine with me.' He gave her a look that made her belly flip over.

'Remember, though, I'm the one with the cuffs.' Damn, she didn't give a shit if she sounded breathless. The idea of having Quinn cuffed to her bed . . . there wasn't enough oxygen on the planet to refill her lungs after that image.

'Yes, you are, and I'll hold you to that.' He chuckled and checked his watch. 'We should have dinner later tonight.'

'My thoughts exactly.' She hesitated on her next words, but then blurted them out. 'We don't have much time left.'

'No, we don't. But there is always after Vegas. This doesn't have to end here.' He stroked his thumb across the delicate skin of her wrist and fire raced through her blood.

Memories of last night flooded her, and Bonni drew in a soft breath. Quinn had passed his crash course in getting to know Bonni Connolly's erogenous zones with flying colors.

'No, it doesn't. But you do push me outside my comfort zone.' She didn't feel the least bit shy admitting this.

'That's a good thing, don't you think?' He nodded and gave her a heartfelt look.

Bonni met his gaze. 'Sometimes. But it can also create a craving in me.'

Quinn laughed softly and pulled her wrist so they were inches apart. 'I have to agree with you there. You are my craving now.'

'I think I like the sound of that,' she whispered. 'So what time should we do dinner later, then? When will you be all mine, after you're free from all this?' She didn't break her gaze from his.

'It depends how well I do.' He pressed his lips to her hair.

'I have confidence in you.' Bonni clutched his arms.

'Keep your phone close, I'll text you. If I'm doing good, it will be later on, between six and seven o'clock. If I do poorly, I'll be done even earlier.'

'Okay. Then I'll bank on seven.' Bonni gave him a look that she hoped showed her confidence in him.

'That's the kind of positivity I need. Throw it out there into the universe and it'll come back to you, right?'

'If you believe in that stuff.' Bonni gave him a sideways glance.

'I guess I believe in whatever is handy at the time.'

'That can work in your favor—'

An announcement came across a speaker and Quinn held up his hand, tilting his head to listen. She wasn't thrilled to be cut off like that and furrowed her brows. Quinn stood and she followed his lead.

'I couldn't understand, is it time for you to go?'

'Yes. I'm sorry. I'm glad you came, even if we only had a short time together.'

'Me too.' Bonni's heart started to beat faster, knowing there were just a precious few minutes left before he went back to his game and she to her day. The anticipation of their dinner later was the only calming influence on her otherwise riotous emotions. She'd never been so unglued by a man before and controlling herself was the hardest thing she'd ever had to do.

Bonni followed Quinn as he carved his way through the growing crowd. A number of people stopped him to shake his hand and congratulate him on advancing to the next round. He was very gracious and polite, while she seethed with frustration. All she wanted to do was drag him out of here. Get him alone, away from all the people, so they could spend time together. These unfamiliar emotions were making her crazy, and she gripped his hand a little tighter.

Quinn turned to her. She looked up at him and, to her horror, she felt the hot swell of threatening tears. *What is the matter with me?* He brushed her hair from her cheek. 'Shh, it's okay, Bonni.'

'I'm sorry, I-I'm . . .' She shook her head, incredulous at her despair. 'I don't know what's wrong with me.'

'I know. I feel it too. But they're waiting for me.' Quinn whispered in her ear. 'How about a kiss for luck?'

She nodded, unable to form any words.

He pulled her behind one of the room's pillars and gathered her in his arms.

'I'm glad you came. And now, with this kiss, I'm guaranteed to win.'

Bonni's mood was immediately lifted by the upbeat tone his voice held. She turned her face to his. 'Talk about pressure. But I can handle it. C'mere.'

His lips took hers and she wrapped her arms around his neck, pressing her body to him. She damn well gave him more than just a kiss for luck. She wanted him to feel her, to remember how their bodies meshed so sweetly. Leave him with the memory of her body next to his, her lips on his, so that he would be burning for her, just as she was for him, with the anticipation for later.

In that perfect moment, she was happy, but the kiss was much too short and, reluctantly, they parted.

'Tonight. Text me.'

'It's a deal.'

Bonni watched him leave, and saw how quickly he immersed himself back into the games. He was assigned a table and took his place. While a number of the other players wore hoodies,

Quinn looked much more polished in his polo. She smiled when he put on his baseball cap, glad that he didn't hide inside a hoodie. He had style and, even in this casual setting, he looked debonair. He cracked his knuckles and placed his palms down on the table. Almost like a pre-game ritual.

The emotion that filled Bonni was quite unfamiliar. Leaving him now, and knowing she'd have to do it again tomorrow, and, if things did move beyond Vegas, that he'd be leaving her whenever he went to a poker game, wherever that might be in the world . . . It was like water on the seed of unease.

Yes, he was a special man, and it surprised the hell out of her that she was thinking beyond Vegas where her relationship with Quinn was concerned. But how could they ever make a relationship outside of Vegas work with their two vastly different careers? Their worlds were very different. Perhaps the chasm between was just too great. The only way to know for sure was for them to have a conversation and lay their cards on the table.

Bonni's phone buzzed in her bag. She knew it would be one of the girls and she was eager to see what they were planning for the rest of the day.

Ceez: *Where r u gurrrl? Wanna get the day started.*

Bons: *Just finished watching Quinn play. He's moving on to the next round. Did you confirm the Canyon tour?*

Ceez: *Yaaas! #vegasbaby Weather is fine.*

Bons: *When do we leave?*

Ceez: *You got 20 minutes to get ur ass back here*

Bons: *Fab! On my way. #funtimes*

Ceez: *Hoover Dam, Grand Canyon #helitour #whompwhomp*

Bonni looked up at Quinn. He was intensely focused on his game. She was glad she'd come to see him. Every little stolen moment together was all they had. She refused to think about the looming inevitability. Excited to see Quinn later, she was now just as eager to spend time with her girls.

She stood and watched him for a few moments. He looked up and Bonni's heart swelled. She blew him a kiss and gave a little wave, mouthing the word 'later'. He didn't smile, keeping his poker face, but he nodded his head, which was good enough for her. She turned and walked swiftly back to the Gladiators. Pushing her concerns aside, if she didn't know better, she would have thought she was walking on air. Bonni hadn't felt this happy in a long, long time and knowing that she was seeing her man later was the icing on the cake.

Chapter 18

Bonni got a kick out of seeing Celia with her face planted against the window of the helicopter. She was like a child, full of enthusiasm and soaking up every little bit of the experience.

'Oh my God, I'd heard seeing the Grand Canyon from the air was the best way.' Celia's voice was muffled, since she was still facing the window.

'This is simply breathtaking.' Fredi was also craning her neck to take everything in, and was busy snapping pictures with her phone. Bonni knew that, at the next quiet moment, Fredi would be sketching up a storm. She had such a creative mind, anything could be inspiration.

Ava was sitting in the front beside the pilot and had a bird's-eye view of their flight path. Ava wasn't the best with heights, but she had flatly refused to be left behind. Her fingers twisted on her seatbelt as the pilot distracted her with historical facts. Bonni had chosen the middle back seat between Celia and Fredi so they could have the better window views.

She already had so many fantastic memories with her besties, and now, here she was creating more. They'd flown over the Hoover Dam, Lake Mead and were now zipping along toward the Canyon. Damn if it hadn't choked her up a little bit.

'I'm glad we booked this tour. Great idea, Celia,' Bonni said into the microphone of the headset she wore. Her friends, and the pilot, all wore a matching set.

Celia turned to hug Bonni, making her even more emotional, so that tears threatened. 'Anything for my girls. We had some pretty damn fine scenery last night at the *Thunder Down Under* show, but these vistas are gorgeous. I just have to bring the kids here one day. I can't wait to show them pictures when I get back.'

'You totally should. California's practically in walking distance.' Bonni tried to keep an upbeat tone to her voice, but the reminder of the rapidly approaching end of their trip saddened her.

Celia was busy taking pictures out of the window and then Instagramming them. 'Hey, Bon-Bon, Fredi, smile!' Celia held her phone up and they all leaned in to each other as best they could so she could snap a selfie. 'Ava, turn around.'

Ava gripped her seatbelt tighter. 'I'm good, thanks.' In an obvious attempt to distract Celia, Ava asked, 'Bonni, what is Quinn doing today?'

'He's still in the tournament. He texted me a selfie at the last break, but I haven't gotten anything in a while, so he must be playing.' Bonni's phone was wedged into her back pocket, but she knew she would feel it vibrate if Quinn texted or called.

Celia focused on her phone, tagging and sending her pictures. 'Eh, it's a good thing he's just a fling. It would never work out with you guys long-term.'

Bonni felt a little shocked and let down. 'Why . . . why would you say that, Celia?'

Still preoccupied with her phone, Celia said, 'Well, c'mon, he's this high-society dude who flits from game to game, and you have a job. In Canada. And there's your dad and everything. What are you going to do, just trust that he's not cheating on you while he's off playing in exotic locations and sit around waiting for him to visit you? You're too smart for that. So take him for a ride then put him back in the stable. That's what I do now.'

Wind blew through the small window on the door Celia sat beside, lifting her long curls off her neck and shoulders. Bonni saw a bruise on her neck and her eyes opened wide before she narrowed them to scrutinize the mark. Celia had a hickey! A quick glance at Fredi and Ava showed they hadn't noticed. Bonni sat back in the seat and wondered where she'd got the love bite from. Then she drew in a soft breath. *Landon!* Bonni had noticed their *connection* last night, and damn! *Celia* had had sex with Landon. Or at least made out with him. But why hadn't the other two picked up on it? Best keep this to herself for now.

'Come on,' Ava interrupted. 'A long-distance relationship could work. You just have to try harder.' Trust Ava to try to put a positive spin on things.

'Aves, why would Bonni possibly waste herself on – ow! Fredi, why did you hit me?' It was impossible for Bonni to miss Fredi smacking Celia on the arm, but she just stared into space. Celia's words only fed into Bonni's concerns. It upset her, and she knew she probably wasn't hiding it very well.

There was a rustling sound, and then Bonni felt Celia take her hand. She looked at her friend, her eyes stinging with unshed tears.

'Oh, Bonni, I'm sorry. Quinn's a good guy, and he's certainly not acting like a dude who's only out for a good time. Maybe Ava's right. Maybe you guys can make things work long distance. Maybe he'll even want to settle down soon. He's not getting any younger, after all.' As reassurances went, Celia failed miserably and Bonni could tell her friend didn't believe a word of it, but she felt lucky to have a bestie who'd support her even when she thought Bonni was being an idiot.

'Okay, you are all getting way ahead of yourselves. Enough.' She wasn't ready to confess to her friends that she was falling for Quinn. And hard. How could she be falling in love with a man she had just met?

But she knew she was.

The pilot cut in, halting any further conversation. 'We'll take one low pass below the canyon rim and then we land. From there, you can access the Skywalk or get some food.'

'I'm going on that Skywalk,' Celia announced. 'Who else?'

'I'm in,' Bonni answered. She saw Ava shaking her head. 'You have to, Ava! You can't come all this way and chicken out.'

'We'll drag you on it if we have to. It'll be the best photo op. I want one of all of us so I can blow it up and put it in my studio,' Fredi told them.

'That would be awesome,' Celia said.

'I'll just close my eyes then.' Ava didn't sound confident at all, and Bonni laughed.

'You'll be fine. Just think, if it collapses, we'll all go together.'

'That's not funny, Bonni!'

Bonni looked out the window and a million thoughts ran through her head. Why was it that when she was away from Quinn her doubts crept back in? Nerves made her feel sick, and the last thing she wanted was to be feeling like that on this trip. Maybe she could meet Quinn later than seven. It would give her time to think some more. As much as it pained her to do it, as the helicopter came in for the landing Bonni texted him the change of plans. Stuffing her phone in her purse, she resolved to have a great day with her friends before potentially saying goodbye to Quinn that night.

Chapter 19

'Hey, man, that was a pretty damn good game. I watched it from the sportsbook.' Landon clapped Quinn on the back and sat on the stool next to him.

'Yeah, whatever. It's a win.' Quinn felt so twisted up inside about Bonni it was hard to be enthusiastic about his victory.

'It got you in the finals tomorrow, though.' The bartender walked over. 'I'll have a Corona, and so will he.' Landon tilted his head toward his brother.

Quinn held up his beer. 'Already got one.'

'Have another.'

'Give me a shot of Jack first.'

Landon looked at him, and Quinn sent him a challenging look back. Landon raised his hands in supplication. 'All right. Drink away.'

The bartender put a shot glass in front of Quinn, filled it with Jack and then slid two bottles of Corona with lime in the top on the bar.

'What's up your ass?' Landon asked him.

'Nothing. What's up yours?' Quinn shot the Jack down in one gulp then grimaced.

'You should've just had the beer.' Landon shook his head, pushed the lime down the neck of the bottle and took a long pull. 'JD will only get you in trouble.'

'Now I'll have the beer. I just needed a jolt of jet fuel.' Quinn pulled his phone out from his pocket and checked it again, then put it down on the counter.

'Did you see her this morning?'

Quinn nodded. 'Yeah, she turned up at the tournament.'

'Sounds a little clingy for a one-night stand. What do you really know about this woman anyway?

Quinn shrugged his shoulders. 'She's beautiful, fantastic in bed. A loyal friend and a devoted daughter. And she's a cop in Canada.'

'A cop? I would've never guessed it.'

'That's exactly what I said.' Quinn lifted the bottle and tipped it, letting the cold liquid slide down his throat. Images flashed through his mind of their night, the way he pushed her up against the windows, naked and exposed. How he'd sunk his cock into her and nearly lost his mind. Sharing their lives in the intimacy of his room. Getting to know her, learning that her beautiful exterior was matched by her beautiful soul. He sighed.

Landon regarded him thoughtfully, the air feeling heavy despite being broken by the noise from the nearby casino. 'Dude, I think you've fallen for her.'

'Don't be stupid. Love at first sight isn't a thing, and I've known her for all of two days.' No way could he admit to his brother that the thought had crossed his mind as well.

'Look, you make your living reading people, instantly sizing them up. When you finally meet "the one", why wouldn't you

know right away? You know I'm right. I can see it in your eyes.'
Landon's phone buzzed, but he ignored it.

Quinn took a few gulps of beer and thought about it. 'All it
was ever meant to be was fun. Nothing more.'

'Maybe that's what you told yourself, but c'mon. You wouldn't
be sitting here drowning your sorrows in beer if Bonni didn't
mean something to you.'

Quinn sighed and shook his head. 'I can't believe we're talking about this. If Dad could see us now, he'd call us a pair of
pussies.'

'Forget about Dad's antiquated notions of masculinity. I'm
your brother. If you can't tell me, who can you tell?'

Quinn gave a sideways look at Landon. 'Fine. I'm starting to
think . . . I mean, maybe I'm wondering if . . . there could be
more. After Vegas. Even though she's a cop, and I can tell she's
not entirely comfortable with gambling.'

Landon straightened and tapped a finger on the bar. 'You
can always consider the alternative.'

'And that is?' Quinn was sceptical, not really sure he wanted
to hear the answer.

'You can always come back into the fold. Become part of
Bryant Enterprises. You know there's a place for you, when
you're ready. Your ability to read people and adapt to situations
on the fly would be of great use to the company.'

'I don't know. The whole reason I left home after high school
was to get away from Dad and his "everything starts and ends
with the company" mentality. I worked too hard to break out of
that mold and be my own man.'

'Dad's not in charge anymore. I am. You've proven you can
make it on your own, without the family fortune, so now you're
just being a stubborn dick. Come back. Work with me. You'd

still have to do some traveling, but there's no reason you can't base out of Canada.'

Quinn found himself considering it. Something he never imagined he'd ever do. Give up his hard-won independence? Go back to the life he'd run far and fast from years ago? Or should he think of it like building a new life, one with Bonni in it? Just forty-eight hours and he was considering making these major changes. It was terrifying.

'Are you seeing her tonight?' Landon asked.

'We were supposed to have dinner at seven but she texted me to push it back. Plans with her friends. I texted her back but she hasn't answered me.'

Landon nodded and indicated to the bartender that they'd need another round. 'Her friends are a lot of fun,' Landon told him.

'To be honest, I really haven't spent a lot of time with them. Been really focusing on Bonni.'

'They must have been a wild group in their college days, because they really know how to party now.' There was something in Landon's tone that made Quinn look sharply at his brother.

'You asshole, you slept with one of them, didn't you?'

Landon took a sip of his beer and didn't meet Quinn's gaze.

'Those are Bonni's friends! How am I supposed to face her when my dickwad of a brother breaks one of her best friends' heart?' Quinn's voice cut through the noise of the bar, causing a few heads to turn in their direction.

Landon pivoted on his stool. 'First off, if I did engage in sexual activity with one of those ladies, rest assured it was consensual and she knew the score. Second, if you weren't thinking long term with Bonni, why would it matter if I messed around with one of her friends?' he said, a knowing tone in his voice.

Quinn shook his head and focused on his beer. 'You are *such* an asshole.' No way would he tell Landon he was right.

Landon picked up his beer and held it out to his brother. 'Here's to women who are worth changing for.'

Quinn looked at his brother and Landon waggled the bottle, waiting. Would he really do it? Would he give up traveling to foreign countries, give up the thrill of living on the turn of a card? For Bonni? Knowing the answer, deep in his gut, he tapped his bottle against Landon's. 'I'm not saying I'm taking the job, but the benefits package better be damn attractive.'

'Oh my God, persnickety, as Mom would say. It's just like when we were kids and you couldn't eat dinner if any of your foods were touching.'

'You're such a ball sack.' Calling him a name from their childhood.

For Bonni, it'd be worth it. And, hopefully, she felt the same way.

Chapter 20

Quinn: *Have fun with your friends. Text me when you're done.*

Bonni read Quinn's reply over again for the millionth time. It read so . . . emotionless. Was he angry? Was he okay with her decision? Did he care? Part of her wanted him to argue and persuade her to stick to their original plan. The other part was relieved he didn't push her. It was all terribly confusing, and she felt like she'd been wrestling with her feelings for Quinn for ages instead of mere days.

Maybe the time away from Quinn would give her some clarity. Help her figure things out. She knew she was sacrificing precious moments with him, but she'd definitely make sure they saw each other tonight. Her gut was telling her they needed to have a talk, to figure out what they were, what they could be. It was so strange that she felt like she'd known him for ever. How could someone have such a swift and significant impact in her life? She wasn't ready to say goodbye to him.

She stared at the phone, her fingers hovering over the keyboard, twitching, and so close to replying. As she had been since he sent the text hours ago. What was there to say?

Do you care if you never see me again?
I feel like meeting you has changed my life.
I think I love you.
Okay, talk to you then.

She sighed and sent her phone to its lock screen. The night had begun with a drink at a piano bar in New York New York. They left the bar via a faux Brooklyn Bridge and wandered the strip until they'd located a Fat Tuesday, home of alcoholic drinks that came in three-feet long to-go cups. They'd each gotten one and taken increasingly tipsy selfies with an increasingly grumpy Ava who insisted she wasn't that short, dammit!

Now the four of them stood on the street and stared up at the Eiffel Tower.

'Wow, it looks so real.' Celia was in awe.

'We can pretend we're in Paris.' Ava sighed. 'It's the city of romance.' She turned to Fredi. 'Why don't you ever do a photo shoot there? I want to go to Paris.'

'Ah, maybe because it costs a lot of money? How could I ever compete with the French couture anyway? And even if I did, who said I'd be taking you with me?'

'To go to Paris, I would sit in the coach and be your gofer. Heck, I know you so well, you wouldn't even need to give me orders. I would just automatically bring you your five o'clock can of Diet Coke.'

'What are you talking about, Fredi? You're a wonderful designer,' Bonni said, wobbling a bit when she leaned back to look at the tower.

Fredi grabbed her arm. 'Whoa there.'

'I'm okay.' Bonni nodded, but didn't look up, just in case she lost her balance again.

'Maybe one day somebody special will take you, Celia.' Ava gave her a nudge.

'Ha! Dickhead was supposed to take me for our tenth anniversary, which would have been last year.' She held up her fingers and counted. 'Yeah. I bet he took the skank.' Her bitter tone turned wistful. 'I always wanted to try those French pastries – I forget what they're called, but the round flat ones and come in pink and blue and yellow?'

'Macarons?' Fredi answered.

'Yes! Do you think they'd have them here somewhere?'

'Let's go in and see if we can find any.' Ava said. 'A friend of mine was here a few years ago and she went on and on about the French patisserie here. If we can't be in the city of love, then we can at least pretend we are.' Ava hooked her elbow through Celia's and led her inside.

'I never really thought of Vegas as a romantic place,' Fredi mused. 'Despite all the hullaboo about quickie weddings.'

Bonni nodded in agreement. 'Me neither, actually. It always seems to have a frenzied feel to it.' They trailed after Ava and Celia to the base of the tower.

Fredi nodded thoughtfully. 'Exactly! Like, if you don't seize the moment, you'll have missed your chance. Act now or, before you know it, you're on a plane back home.'

Bonni felt off balance again, as everything seemed to keep going for her, tilting her a little bit, and she looked down at the Fat Tuesday cup she was still carrying. Fredi's words landed like a punch to the gut and she wondered suspiciously if Fredi was trying to sneakily give her advice.

But now Fredi was wondering aloud about the marketability

of wedding dresses that could be converted to cocktail dresses, for brides who got married on a whim or eloped.

'—like, a detachable train, maybe. And then perhaps there'd be a way to convert the veil into a matching drawstring purse.'

'Fredi! Bonni!' Ava yelled to them. 'We have to get tickets.'

Bonni began to move past her, reaching for her wallet.

'No, you're not. No way.' Ava held her ground. 'You've spent too much already. Down-payment-on-a-house money, remember? This is on me.' A few minutes later she waved the tickets. 'Okay, we're good to go.'

At the top, they were able to see the whole strip.

'This view is the same as our hotel, only from a different angle,' Fredi pointed out.

'Yes, but it's from the top of the Eiffel Tower.' Wistful longing echoed in Celia's voice again.

Bonni wondered if Quinn had ever been to Paris. Had he stood at the top of the real Eiffel Tower with a glamorous beauty on his arm? One who wore designer dresses effortlessly and didn't assess every person she met for a potential threat. Fredi had wandered over to a bench and was now scribbling in her sketchbook, likely working on her elopement wedding dresses ideas. Celia was now playing around with the straw in her drink and taking slightly obscene selfies. Bonni really hoped she wasn't sending them to Landon.

Ava came up next to her. 'You doing okay, Bonni?'

'Yeah. It's just been so great spending time with you guys, I'm sad that it's almost over.' Bonni crossed her arms over her chest, nearly bonking her chin with the Fat Tuesday glass as she leaned against the railing.

'This is all about creating memories. Everything we do, we'll remember later on in life. So we need to enjoy each moment,'

Ava said. 'Besides, it's not like we'll never see each other again. Unless, of course, it's not us you're worried about saying goodbye to.'

'This trip *is* all about memories,' Bonni said. First Quinn, and now Ava talking about memories. Memories are what carry us, and now she was realizing it even more. So, even if she never got to see Quinn again, even if their talk tonight didn't go the way she hoped it would, she would always remember him. Ava shifted over and wrapped an arm around Bonni's shoulders, and she leaned into her friend. 'C'mon, bitches, the hunky employee said there's a bakery in the lobby. Mama wants some macarons!' Celia's exuberant cry broke the moment and Ava gave Bonni a final squeeze before they turned to face their friend.

To keep herself from reaching for her phone again, Bonni sucked on the straw of the drink, but got nothing except empty cup. She desperately needed another one. Somehow, she had to put Quinn – and their inevitable conversation – out of her mind for now, and the only possible way to do that was booze. A lot of it. 'I need to find another Fat Tuesdays,' Bonni announced, holding up the empty cup.

'I think we're in for a night, ladies.' Fredi nodded knowingly and hustled Bonni into the elevator. 'Don't forget, there is now a dual wager . . . a Bonni Pukes pool and a Celia Pukes pool, both still active and acting wagers.'

The strip was with humming with people and Bonni spied a Margaritaville.

'Oh! It's five o'clock somewhere! We *have* to go have a margarita and a cheeseburger in paradise. Fin's Up!'

'I have no idea what you're talking about,' Fredi said, while Celia belted out the song lyrics in a decent alto.

'That's because you only listen to classical music and boy

bands.' Bonni found four seats at the bar and ordered them each a margarita. 'Jimmy Buffett style, kind sir,' she said to the bartender. Bonni planned to give her future self an epic hangover to drown out the pain of her likely-soon-to-be-broken heart.

Chapter 21

Quinn's room seemed empty. When Bonni was here yesterday, her presence had permeated every corner. Now, it was just a big, cold, empty hotel room. Gone was the color, the life. *Her*.

He shook his head and finally admitted what he'd been holding back since Landon had broached the subject earlier that day.

He was falling for her. It astounded him that, in the few short days since they'd met, when she wasn't with him, the gaping hole in his life was painfully evident.

Walking over to the mini-fridge, Quinn grabbed a beer and twisted off the cap, tossing it on the counter. He wondered again what she was doing. She still hadn't texted him. The night ahead seemed endless.

He'd just watch the hockey game, to distract himself. He had no burning desire to go out to any bars.

He didn't want anyone else. He wanted Bonni. If only she'd get here, so he could tell her so.

Quinn dropped on to the desk chair and propped his feet up

on the corner of the desk. Placing the beer on the floor, he grabbed the remote and started cruising through channels out of boredom. He finally changed the channel to the game.

His phone buzzed against the desk and Quinn lunged for it, knocking it to the floor.

'Shit.' Scooping it up, disappointment swept through him at the message on the screen. It was Landon. Not Bonni.

Golden Child: *U heard from her?*

Q: *No. Watching the game.*

Golden Child: *Come to the bar. Game's playing on one of the screens and there's plenty of fish in this sea.*

Quinn shook his head. Being around other people was the last thing he wanted to do.

Q: *Nope.*

Golden Child: *Want company?*

Q: *No, stay there. At least one of us should have a good time tonight.*

Golden Child: *Bro, I'm sure she'll text.*

Not feeling like getting into it with his brother, Quinn put his phone back on the desk. His mind kept drifting back to Bonni.

He should text her, flat out ask her if she was still coming by, but what if she was ghosting him? As long as he didn't ask, there was always the possibility that she was still coming. And he wasn't entirely ready to have *that* conversation. Quinn couldn't even figure out how he'd start it.

Hi, Bonni, glad you're not ghosting me. Now that you're finally here, I wanted to let you know that I think I'm falling in love with you and I want to give up my livelihood so I can follow you home to Canada, but don't worry about having to support me because I'm going to work for my brother in the family company and take the job I've resisted taking for the last fifteen years. Whaddya say?

Fuck.

As much as he wanted her to be with him, he would never try to pressure her to do something she didn't want to do. That's how a guy winds up with jail time and a restraining order, and rightly so.

Quinn didn't want to scare Bonni. He wanted to love her.

Double fuck. Who the hell was he right now?

Near the end of the second period, there was a roaring fight. He moved to the end of the bed and leaned closer to watch. On the desk, his phone buzzed again, but he ignored it, figuring it was probably Landon again, and shouted at the television.

'What are you thinking? Now they've got a power play! Damn idiots.'

At the commercial, he took his empty bottle to the recycling bin and grabbed another one, muttering about the stupidity of the hockey players and sitting back down in time for the face-off. He got caught up watching the game for another few minutes before remembering his phone.

He sat upright when he saw it was a text from Bonni.

'What the fuck?' Quinn turned his phone, trying to view the image she'd sent. It looked like an attempt at a selfie, but it was a disaster. He could see her friends on the fringe of the picture, the side of her head, her hair and her mouth, wide open, laughing.

Quinn smiled, as just seeing her face in the pic made his heart swell. He was glad she was having a good time, and happy that he'd obviously crossed her mind and she'd sent the photo. But he missed her. The whole point of this trip had been for her to spend time with her friends, and he would never try to come between them, but he wanted her here, with him. His heart tightened, and he wished that, at the very least, he was there having laughs right alongside them.

Another buzz and another photo. Sideways again, but this time she was blowing a kiss into the camera. He chuckled.

'She's got to be drunk texting,' he told the empty room. Quinn typed back to her. *Take care of yourself, darlin'. Have fun and don't get into any trouble. Still hoping to see you tonight.*

He had the urge to include a heart and, if he hadn't admitted that he was falling for her, that would've been a clear sign that he was a goner. She didn't answer and, eventually, he put the phone down. He kept it close, though, just in case she messaged him again. All she had to do was beckon and he would come running.

Chapter 22

Fredi and Celia were running offense, clearing the way, as Ava struggled behind them with Bonni.

'I don't think I've ever seen her this way,' Fredi said, keeping her arm in front of her to ward off people. '*This* is why men are not worth the trouble.'

'I haven't either. I hope she doesn't get alcohol poisoning or anything.' Celia looked back over her shoulder with concern. 'How did she get this bad?'

'I have no idea. It has to be those banana banshee things she was drinking. I think they were super-strong.'

Bonni heard her friends talking, but it was like they were under water, and her eyes kept crossing. She blinked.

'Ava.' Bonni turned her head and loudly whispered into her ear.

'Yes, Bonni.'

'I want to see Quinn.'

'I think you should just go to bed.'

'No, I need to see him. Bad.' Bonni had to make Ava

understand that it was important for her see Quinn, they had a date, but she knew she needed help getting up to his room.

'Don't you think you've had too much to drink? Do you really want to see him in this condition?'

'Yes. It's our last night.' Bonni nodded, and her head dropped on to Ava's shoulder. 'Please, help me get to his room.'

'How about you guys go up? I'll take her to Quinn and then bring her to the room if he doesn't want to deal with her drunk ass,' Ava said to Fredi and Celia.

'Okay,' Celia said. 'But if she throws up in the hotel, I should get all the money in the Celia Pukes pool.'

The women separated and Ava got Bonni into the elevator, coaxing Quinn's room number from her. Once the elevator started moving, Bonni asked Ava, 'You like Celine Dion, right?'

Ava brushed the hair out of Bonni's face and tried to tidy her friend up a bit. 'How does anyone not like Celine Dion?'

Bonni's eyes widened. 'I know, right? Oh my God, Ava, did you know she's here in Vegas? We should totally go see her.' Overcome with fangirl delight, Bonni was suddenly struck with the need to sing 'My Heart Will Go On'.

Ava tried futilely to shush her for several floors, and then Bonni grabbed her arm and shook it. 'Ava, Aves, Jack, he died! It was so sad! Rose is a selfish bitch. She should've let him climb on the door. If it were Quinn, I would *totally* let him share my door. I wouldn't want him to *die*. Ava, Ava, I think I love him. Are we in a romcom? You would tell me if we were in a movie, right?'

'Oh, Lord, Bonni, you're a right mess. I haven't seen you this drunk since that Ponzi scheme guy committed suicide before you could get all the money back to his victims. Are you *sure* you want to see Quinn?'

'That guy, Ava, listen, this is really important,' Bonni said.

'That guy was an *asshole*. Quinn is not an asshole, though. He's amazing. Amazeballs. Balls of amazing. We have stuff in common and his dick, Ava, *listen*, his dick—'

'Thank God we're alone in this elevator,' Ava said.

Bonni wasn't sure why her friend was looking quite so desperate, but she felt the need to continue sharing this very important information. Oh, Quinn. They were supposed to talk tonight. She was going to sit him down and have a very sensible conversation about expectations and feelings and commitments and boundaries, but her carefully rehearsed words had dissolved upon application of alcoholic banana-slushy goodness. All she knew now was that she loved him. Near, far, wherever he was, her heart would go on. She should sing again.

Bonni picked up where she had left off as the elevator whooshed to a stop and the door opened. Ava put her hands on Bonni's shoulders and guided her out. She tried once again to shush Bonni, but Bonni knew – she just *knew* – that love had touched them one time and that it would last for a lifetime.

Ava muttered, 'The things I do for true love.'

As quickly as she could, Ava brought Bonni to Quinn's door, but hesitated while Bonni continued to sing. 'Bonni, it's not too late to turn around. I can text him from your phone, explain what happened—'

'No.' Bonni pounded on the door with her fist. 'Open up, it's the police. The looooove police.' She giggled.

'Bonni! Let's really try to not wake up the entire hotel, okay?'

The door opened, and Quinn stood there. 'What the hell – oh, holy shit, what do have we here?'

He was so pretty. Bonni was so lucky that she'd found such a pretty man. She stopped singing so she could stare at the very pretty man. He should be in a museum so that everyone could see how pretty he was. No, that wouldn't work, because then she'd have to share him, and she didn't want to do *that*.

Ava said wryly, 'A very drunk Bonni insisted she was going to keep your date.'

'Because he's so pretty! But I'm not sharing!' Bonni reached her hands out to Quinn and he took them, helping her keep her balance when she wobbled a little.

'I'm sorry, Quinn. She was relentless. I hope you don't mind. I mean, she's just smashed. I can take her back to our suite, but she was determined—'

Quinn reached for Bonni's waist and gathered her into his arms. 'It's fine, Ava. I'm glad you brought her. Don't worry, I'll take care of her.'

'Quinn?' Bonni looked up at him. 'I don't want you to be in a museum. Can we have our date instead?'

He smiled down at her and she leaned into his touch when he cupped her face. 'We can. That's why Ava brought you to me.'

'She did? Aww, she's one of my best friends, you know. I love all my besties equally, but Ava's the best bestie.' Her tone was very earnest as she made sure Quinn knew how awesome Ava was.

'Yes, clearly she's the best, if she helped you keep our date.' Quinn's eyes were smiling, and Bonni couldn't help but smile back.

From over her shoulder, she heard, 'Bonni, are you still sure you want to burden Quinn with your drunk-ass self?'

'Yes, he's my main man, Ava.' Bonni snuggled into Quinn. Not only was he pretty, he was warm and cuddly!

'Okay, Quinn, good luck. Also, I know people in the IRS. If you hurt her, not Landon or God Almighty will be able to save you from having your entire life audited.' Ava was using her fierce voice. Bonni made a little 'grr' noise then giggled again.

Quinn's arm tightened around her waist. 'Understood. I'll take care of her, and we'll connect in the morning. And, Ava, don't worry. I have a feeling I'm the one that's going to be hurting,' he replied.

'You smell so good, I could just eat you up.' Bonni's words were muffled by his neck. She vaguely heard Ava say good night, and then Quinn was closing the door and shuffling her inside. Suddenly, his last words registered with her and she pulled back, needing to tell him something urgently.

'We need to talk. I had this whole big script and things I wanted to say, but I got all tangled up and I got drunk, and now all that really matters is that I tell you that my heart will go on, if yours does, Quinn. I'm all in.'

The next thing Bonni knew, Quinn was hugging her tightly, and she buried her face in his chest, marveling again at his yumminess. Then she remembered something else.

'Quinn, listen, Quinn, this is really important.' She grabbed his face with her hands, forcing him to look into her eyes. 'Quinn, if I get sick tonight, don't tell Celia.'

Chapter 23

'Let's get you a drink of water.' Quinn scooped Bonni up into his arms and carried her further into the room. He sat her on the couch, putting a pillow behind her back when she started to slide.

'I don't want to drink water. Do you have more champagne? Sometimes it tastes yucky but, in Vegas, it's *awesome*!' Quinn watched Bonni try to look around the room, but her eyes crossed and she started to tilt again.

'I think it's better we have water.'

She stuck out her tongue and wrinkled her nose. 'But you can have water *anywhere*.'

Quinn thought his heart was going to explode at how cute she was being. Her head fell back and he wondered what on earth had made her hell-bent on getting so drunk. 'Baby, Las Vegas water is filled with magic and luck, so you gotta drink it all up. You just stay there while I get it.' Quinn moved quickly to the bathroom to fill two glasses from the tap before Bonni decided she could fly, or something equally nonsensical.

'Here you go, darling. Drink up now.' He sat beside her and she slumped into him. Lifting her to a sitting position, he held a glass to her mouth. She gulped some water down and he wiped a drop off her chin. Bonni looked up at him, her eyes, normally so alert and vibrant, now glassy. She was having a hard time keeping them open. While he was appreciative of her adorableness, he wished he'd pushed harder for dinner. If he had, perhaps she wouldn't have gotten so drunk. What was bothering her?

'I'm going to miss you, Quinn.' Her breath caught.

'Where am I going? Here, you need to drink some more.'

Bonni drank the rest of the water, wiping her hand over her mouth, and he gently placed her back on to the pillows.

'You're going to leave,' she said, and he watched her eyes flutter.

Cupping her face again, he traced the curve of her cheek. 'I'm not going anywhere. I'm here with you right now.'

'I don't want you to go, Quinn.'

He shifted the pillows around so he could sit at the corner of the couch, and drew her back on him. 'I don't want to go either.'

'You're special. I like you, a lot.'

She was telling him things he wanted to hear. Only she was drunk. Perhaps talking truth?

'I'm not going to go anywhere. You'll stay here with me tonight.'

Bonni snuggled into him and rested her cheek on his chest. ''Kay. I can hear your heart beat.'

He brushed her hair off her face again and saw that her eyes were closed. He wrapped his arm around her shoulder and held her tight. Quinn stayed that way for a little while, cradling her.

Then she suddenly sat up, startling him.

'Are you okay, baby? Did you fall asleep?'

She shook her head. 'Nope. Just resting my eyes. Everything is spinning.'

'I'm not surprised. You've had a lot to drink.'

'Yup. Gotta forget stuff sometimes, ya know?'

He was silent for a minute, then asked, 'What are you trying to forget?'

Bonni shrugged her shoulders. 'All the people going away.'

'Who's going away?'

'Everybody does, you know. So I decided I would always leave first. I wouldn't ever get left behind again.'

He needed to steer her off that path, even though she'd revealed an important character trait about herself. Would she leave him? Run away? *Does she think I'll leave her?*

'Not everybody will leave you. I won't leave you.' Quinn felt his stomach sink. Because leaving was what a professional poker player did. Constantly traveling to follow the games. He knew, in that moment, that if he wanted to be with Bonni he'd have to give it up.

'My mom did, she didn't like all of Daddy's traveling. So . . . poof. Gonzo. She was there when Doug got in trouble, they got him help, but as soon as he was clean, she left. Birthday and Christmas cards, that's it. Doug didn't think about me when he chased his addiction, and he didn't think about me when he decided he had to move to get away from bad habits and triggers. He left too. He calls sometimes. Mostly, it was just me and Daddy.'

Quinn felt a surge of anger at her family for abandoning her, for choosing their own interests over Bonni. He could almost understand why her brother had done it, but her mother? Then:

'You have your dad. He's been there for you.'

'Yes, and no.' Her voice was low and pained.

'How's that? It can't be both.'

She nodded with exaggeration. 'Yes, it can.' She shifted and looked into his eyes. The expression in them was new, sadness mixed with pain . . . and anger. She poked her finger hard at her chest. '*I* know. You can't tell me I don't know. Because I do.'

'I'm confused, babe, explain it to me.'

'My dad. He's here, but he's not here.' She waved her hand. 'Not *here*, but, oh, I don't know.' She drew in a ragged breath. 'He's in Virginia. Locked up, in a place . . . his mind.'

Quinn began to feel Bonni's despair as she grappled for words. He remained silent, letting her find her way. He sensed this was a big deal, telling him about her father, and he wanted to let her say it at her own pace.

'H-he, doesn't know me anymore. He's forgotten me and our life. Everything. And he was everything to me. He taught me self-defense and how to shoot a gun, but he also took me shopping for a prom dress. Friday nights, we'd watch old Westerns and eat popcorn and he'd tell me that a true hero does things because the cause is just, not for money or fame. And he doesn't remember *any* of it.'

Things were starting to click into place, and all Quinn could do was hold her. His heart surged. 'Bonni—'

She put her hand up. 'Stop, I wasn't finished . . . not finished.' Her eyes filled with tears and her chin wobbled. Quinn's heart broke for her and he tightened his embrace, hoping his presence would give her the comfort she needed.

'I'm sorry, Bonni. So sorry.'

A big fat tear dripped down her check. Quinn swiped it away, having to swallow back his own emotion and the rawness of hers. Never before had he been so ripped open. Seeing her like this moved him to his core.

'Oh, Quinn. I miss him so much! It's so horrible to see who he is now. He's no man, just a shell, with my dad lost inside with that terrible, terrible disease, and I'll never get him back. Never!' She buried her face into his chest and her tears soaked his shirt.

'Tell me, Bonni, I'm here for you.'

Bonni pushed up, pulling back from him a little, with cheeks stained with tears and a serious tone in her voice. 'But are you really, Quinn? Or will you leave too, gone off to the next poker game? Or will you go away little by little, like Daddy did?'

This was the perfect moment to tell her that he wanted to move to Canada, that he was ready to work for Bryant Enterprises and stop gambling, but the words just wouldn't come. 'I'm here now.'

'I was there too. But I was afraid. So I left.' She plucked at the button on his shirt.

'Left where, darling?'

'Left Virginia and went to Toronto. I couldn't bear to see him fade away and so I left!' She looked up at him, her hair mussed, eyes rimmed red and lips swollen. Never had he thought she looked more beautiful and vulnerable, and all he wanted to do was keep her safe, happy and protected.

'Your job took you there, didn't it?'

'Yes, but I didn't have to go.' She sniffled. 'I ran away from him when he needed me most, Quinn! I lost those last precious, lucid days with him, that I can never get back, because I wasn't strong enough!'

'Baby, calm down. Shh, it's okay.'

She shook her head and he placed his hands on either side of her face, looking deep into her eyes, stilling her frantic emotions. 'Your father raised you to be an amazing woman, and I'm sure all he wanted was for you to be happy and live your life. You went to Canada to catch bad guys and make the world a better place. I'm sure he is so proud of you.'

Bonni sucked in rapid breaths and slowly calmed down. 'You really think so? I visit him sometimes and tell him about cases I've worked on, and I swear, sometimes it feels like he hears me.'

'The next time you visit, I'll go with you. I'll take you, and I'll be there for you.' It hadn't been a conscious decision to say those words, but Quinn found that he meant them.

'You would do that with me?'

'Yes, I would go with you.' It was a promise Quinn knew he had to keep, because, if he didn't, then he'd be just as bad as the rest of the people who had left her over the years.

She searched his face and smiled a little, before turning away. 'I'm thirsty, and I need to use the restroom,' Bonni murmured.

Quinn helped her from the couch. She wrapped her arm around his waist and he led her to the bedroom. 'You go on in there, and I'll get you another glass of water.'

He watched her drop her purse and phone on the bedside table and hold the wall as she went into the bathroom and closed the door behind her. He stood for a few minutes, watching the closed door, reeling. He felt like he'd been ripped through a hedge backwards and shook his head. How raw must she be feeling?

A few minutes later she came out and flopped on to the bed. He could see she had washed her face and had tried to do something with her hair, as it was a bit damp.

'C'mere.' Bonni reached a hand to him and looked at him through sleepy eyes. He couldn't resist her. Even in her drunken stupor, he thought she was amazing.

'You're taking such good care of me.' She looked up at him and smiled. 'You'd make someone a good husband.'

Quinn laughed. 'I don't know about that. Not many women would put up with me.'

'I'd put up with you.' She reached up and took his face in her hands and pulled him down to her. 'I want you to kiss me, Quinn. Make me feel good. Like you did last night.'

Quinn wasn't about taking advantage of drunk women. But he did kiss her. He'd been longing to all day.

She moaned into his mouth, and her hands were at the waistband of his jeans. 'Let's make love.' She shifted her position and tried to straddle his hips, finally managing to sit on him, rather precariously. He held her hips so she wouldn't topple over but sucked in a sharp breath when she rocked against him. After their time together, he knew the signs of her arousal, and she was setting off all the alarms now.

'Bonni, honey, not tonight.' It was one of the hardest things Quinn had ever had to do. He wanted to make love to her more than life itself, but instead he gently untangled her from him and pulled the sheets back. 'How about we get you undressed and into bed?'

'But I don't want to go to sleep. I want to be with you.'

'And there's nothing more that I want either. But I'd rather you be buzzed on me sober than drunk. No way will I ever take advantage of you.'

Her eyes started to drift closed as he swiftly undressed her. 'You're such a good guy. I'm lucky I met you.'

He didn't have another chance to say anything as her eyelids fell shut. He could tell she'd started dozing by the change in her breathing.

Quinn stood beside the bed and watched her. She was beautiful, her hair tumbling around her on the pillow, the dark of her lashes curving against her flawless skin and her lips, bare of lipstick, slightly open, lush, and he ached to kiss her again. 'No, Bonni,' he whispered in the quiet room, 'I'm the lucky one.'

He turned off the light, shucked his clothes and climbed in

beside her. He pulled her into the crook of his arm and held her, listening to her breathe and loving the feel of her next to him.

Bonni was restless, though, and stirred, her body soft and warm next to him. Quinn held his breath when she placed her hand on his belly. He didn't want to rebuff her, but he had no intention of making love to her while she was drunk. He wanted her to remember his touches, kisses, what it felt like when he moved inside her. Right now, he doubted she'd remember anything, and he realized that he wanted her to remember. Wanted her to know she'd shared something brutally emotional with him. Wanted her to know that he was here for her. If she didn't remember . . . well, he didn't even want to consider that possibility.

Her hand slid lower, her fingers cool and soft on his cock, and she curled them around him. Quinn drew in a sharp breath and closed his eyes. He reached down and gently took her hand in his, lacing their fingers.

'Go to sleep, Bonni. I want no regrets for either of us in the morning,' he whispered, and kissed the top of her head.

'No, let's . . . I want you. I've missed you so much today.' Her sleepy voice slurred her words but held an intimate and sexy tone.

She molded her body to his, her breasts pressing sweetly into his side, her shapely leg draped over his thigh. Quinn bit his lip as the heat of her seared his hip.

He shifted a bit so that he could move her back into the crook of his arm and relieve the temptation. He brushed the hair from her face. Her eyes were still closed, and her perfect white teeth dented the pink of her lower lip. He longed to kiss her.

'You're so sleepy. Let me tell you a bedtime story.' He needed to distract himself as much as he could in order to resist her subtle invitation.

'Mmm, 'kay.' She rested her head on his chest, and he swirled his fingertips over her shoulder and back. Her breath was like a cool whisper over his chest.

'A long time ago, there were two brothers who did everything together. They were as opposite as day and night, but they were best friends. As they grew, they were groomed to go into the family business.'

Her breathing grew a little shallower. She was falling asleep.

Quinn rested his head back on the pillow and closed his eyes. Images of Landon and him, when they were younger, played like a movie in his brain.

'More story,' Bonni murmured.

'Their father had high expectations for them. They were to learn the business, help it expand and make it even more formidable. It was all about profits and money. But to do that would mean they'd have to give up who they were, what they wanted in life.'

Bonni shifted, and her arm tightened across his belly.

'One brother refused. He rebelled and set out to create his own fortune in a very unorthodox way. The other brother did as was expected. But the burden of being responsible for the family is a heavy one, and it weighed on his mind. He was respected, successful and powerful, but he never knew who he could trust and always suspected those around him of wanting something.

'Each year, the brothers would meet up anywhere they could in the world. The brother in the family business supported his brother in everything he did, but he never gave up on the idea that his brother would join the company. But the rebellious brother continued to refuse, not wanting to be hemmed in by corporate life and the trappings of a wealthy lifestyle, still determined to make his own way in life. But then he met a girl.

A girl who, in a very short space of time, turned his world upside down.'

'She did?' Bonni's voice was soft and slurry.

'Yes, she did. So now the rebellious brother is thinking of changing his ways. Doing something that he's never wanted to do in order to be with his lady.'

'That's sweet. But he should be who he wants to be,' she murmured against his chest.

That floored him. It was clear by now that Bonni had no filter when she drank, so she meant it. That was the innocent opinion of a drunk and nearly asleep woman. The insight was powerful, and he realized he didn't really know what to do.

But maybe the question was who did he want to be? Quinn the elite poker player? Or Quinn, Bonni's man? It was a question for the morning.

'Shush, baby, it's time to sleep.' Quinn fixed the covers, making sure she was tucked in and cozy. Soon he heard her breathing become deep and steady. It lulled him, and he drifted off, with Bonni safe in his arms.

Chapter 24

'Hey, baby.' A deliciously sexy voice woke her up. Right along with some deliciously wonderful lips.

'Mmm.' Bonni smiled. 'I could get used to waking up like this every morning.'

'And I could get used to waking you up like this every morning.'

Bonni opened her eyes, squinting at the bright sun pouring in the windows. Quinn was sitting on the edge of the bed, putting on his shoes. 'Are you leaving?'

He turned to press a soft kiss to her lips again. 'Yes, I gotta go. Final rounds today.'

'Nooo, not yet.' Bonni had a flash of déjà vu. Once again, she was trying to coax Quinn into staying while he already had one foot out the door.

'Darling, I'm sorry. I would stay if I could, believe me. But, listen, we really need to talk. Can you come to the tournament and hang out today? You can watch me win and then we can talk afterwards.'

Bonni sat up and grasped his hand. 'But my plane leaves this afternoon. I can't just not be on it. Why don't we talk now?'

Quinn pressed a kiss to the back of her hand. 'There's not enough time. I want us to have a real conversation, where we're both sober, preferably some place without a bed to distract us. Just reschedule your flight to leave tomorrow or the next day. C'mon, be spontaneous. I change flights on a whim all the time.'

He gave her hand a squeeze and then got up, acting like the matter had been settled. What, she was supposed to drop everything, completely change her plans, so she could sit around and wait for him? For a conversation that couldn't be incredibly important if he wasn't making time for it now? Because it was no big deal for him to randomly change his flights to go whenever he wanted, wherever he wanted? Because it was no big deal for him to just *leave*?

Chills ran down Bonni's spine. Tossing the covers off, she stood a little too quickly. She wobbled and pressed her fingertips to her temples, wanting to ease the pounding inside her skull.

'Steady.' Quinn reached for her, and Bonni raised her hand, stopping him.

'No. Don't touch me.'

He froze, a confused expression on his face.

'Not all of us can go where the wind takes us, with no thought to anything. Some of us have actual jobs and actual homes and people who count on us. We can't just flit around the world to play a stupid game.'

Quinn's confusion solidified into coldness, but he took a breath before he said in a measured tone, 'Bonni, maybe you don't remember last night, but it's not what you think—'

Bonni turned away, unable to listen. She yanked on her clothes, grabbed her purse and phone and, as she headed for the door, she said over her shoulder, 'I remember last night perfectly. Being rebellious only gets you so far, Quinn. At some point, you have to grow the fuck up.'

'Bonni, where—'

The door slammed behind her, cutting Quinn's words off. Bonni felt as if she were dying. Her body wouldn't work as it should; her vision blurred and darkened and she gasped for breath. With her hand on the wall, she felt her way to the elevator. It was all she could do to put one foot in front of the other and not fall into a heap.

She had to get moving. Quinn could come out at any time. To head for the tournament . . . or to chase after her? She fled down the hall and punched the elevator call button. The *ding* and swoosh of the elevator doors opening gave her the escape route she needed. Once inside, she took a deep breath and pushed her floor. The doors closed, sealing her in. She was safe.

She was alone.

He hadn't come racing after her. And she wasn't entirely sure he should have. Tears pricked her eyes as she began to realize the magnitude of her actions. She had taken something precious, an emotional intimacy, and thrown it back in his face. Sadness punched her in the heart and she leaned back against the wall, watching the floor numbers indicating the rapid ascent of the elevator.

Was this a break-up? How could it be a break-up when this was just a fling? Bonni scoffed to herself. A fling? What she'd just destroyed, it had been more than just a fling. And she hadn't taken a leap of faith, she hadn't fought for it. No. She had run.

With a chime, the elevator doors slid open and Bonni found herself staring at the painting hanging across the way. The colors blurred as her eyes again welled with tears. Stumbling out of the elevator, she mindlessly made her way down the short corridor to the suite.

Bonni hesitated before opening the door, running the back of her hand across her eyes. She was coming unglued, on the verge of losing it. Now, more than ever, she needed her friends. She needed their understanding. She needed people she could let go with and know they would support her. Entering the room, Bonni closed the door and leaned against it. She took a few deep breaths, trying to calm herself down as much as possible. It was no use.

Pushing herself from the door, she was both shocked and relieved at the chaotic state of the living room. It helped distract her. Clothes, liquor bottles, half-packed suitcases and make-up were strewn about as if a hurricane had hit the room. Their check-out time was late, 1 p.m., but clearly, they were already packing.

'Where are you guys?' she called out.

No one answered her, but she could hear activity in the other rooms. She smiled and was relived her friends, at least, had enjoyed their Vegas vacation. While she had spent the time getting her heart torn into shreds and worrying about a future with a man that likely would never settle down. She was so damn confused, she felt like a train wreck about to happen.

'Hey, Bons, you're back already?' Fredi had been in the kitchenette. She came around with a big glass of orange juice and handed it to her.

'I was going to make Mimosas, but you're so pale. Looks like you could use this instead.'

Bonni nodded and took the glass. 'Thanks. Yeah, I needed to be here with you guys. I've been such a . . .'

'What's wrong, sweetie?'

Bonni grappled for the right words to explain why she was

so upset, but she couldn't find them so she gulped down the orange juice instead.

'Well, I can see something's got you wound up. Come on, let's sit down.' Fredi led her to the couch and sat beside her, pushing Celia's carry-on suitcase to the floor with a thump.

The door to Ava's room opened and she came out with a robe on. 'Oh, honey, are you feeling sick? Did you have a bad night? I knew you shouldn't have gone to see him.'

Bonni shook her head. 'No, the night was fine. Quinn was great. I'm feeling a little rough, but that's to be expected.' She gave her friends an intense look. 'Why did you let me get that trashed?'

Fredi and Ava looked at each other and raised their eyebrows in concern.

'It wasn't us,' Fredi told her. 'It was all you. Celia even tried to stop you from getting another Fat Tuesday refill and you told her that Bon Jovi was overrated. She didn't talk to you for the rest of the night.'

Bonni shook her head. 'I can't believe I let myself get that bad.' She looked up at Ava, feeling like a pathetic mess. 'I just don't know what I'm doing.'

Ava sat beside her and the three of them cuddled on the couch. 'Why don't you tell us what happened?'

Bonni's grief welled up yet again and, this time, she couldn't stop the tears from spilling down her cheeks. 'I can't believe how emotional I am. And what a bitch I was to him.'

'Of course you're emotional, you're in love. It hits you like a train, no doubt about it. Love changes your perspective on life, so naturally you feel unsettled,' Ave soothed.

Ava's words hit Bonni like a bolt of lightning and she was no longer able to deny the truth. *I do! I love him. I love him and that's why the thought of being without him is completely terrifying.*

'You being a bitch?' Fredi shook her head. 'I don't believe that for a minute. You can be tough, yes, but a bitch, never.'

'I was. The things I said as I walked out on him. Oh, God, I've probably ruined everything.'

'Wait, you walked out on Quinn?' Ava asked.

'Yesss, I did, and I left scorched earth in my wake. He tried to talk to me and I didn't even give him a chance.'

Ava and Fredi were silent, and Bonni dropped her face into her hands, her shoulders shaking.

'Stop crying, or I'll be next. Come on. Stop, Bons,' Ava begged her. 'You don't cry, you never cry.'

'I knew you were getting hooked,' Fredi said, shaking her head.

'Fredi! This isn't the time,' Ava scolded her as she rubbed Bonni's back.

Bonni looked at Fredi and she shrugged her shoulders. 'Well, it's true. I meant what I said in the spa, about just enjoying the moment, but I knew you were already too far gone.'

'But everything was so great. Great!' Bonni whispered. 'I'm not just talking about the sex. There was just something about him that spoke to me. Like he's deep down inside of me.'

'Tell us exactly what happened. I'm sure it can be fixed,' Ava encouraged.

Bonni's bedroom door opened and Celia flounced out, wearing one of the hotel's plush robes, her hair all piled on top of her head. She came in like a hurricane, and the room pumped with her energy. For such a little woman, she certainly did have a big aura.

Celia scooped up Fredi's tote from the chair across from the sofa and dropped it on the floor with a careless thud. She crossed her legs carefully, adjusting the robe over her knees. 'That is the best jacuzzi tub ever! I would apologize for using it, but you owed me for the blasphemy you spouted last night about Bon Jovi. Besides, I thought you'd be out with Mr Sexy.' Then Celia furrowed her brow, finally picking up on the mood in the room. 'What's happened? Why are you here?'

Fredi rolled her eyes. 'Bonni was just about to tell us when you barged into the room like an F5 tornado.'

Celia sat back and adjusted the belt on her robe. 'I'm sorry, Bon-Bon. We're all here now. What's going on?'

'He'll never settle down. He just changes his flights, on a whim. He says he does that sort of thing all the time. What's the big deal? he says. Well, it is a big deal! How can you begin a life with someone who will just up and leave whenever he feels like it? I can't just not get on my flight this afternoon.' Bonni's voice trembled. 'I can't do that. It's irresponsible. I have a job to get back to. So I said some things as I walked out the door.'

Bonni jumped up and began pacing, needing to work off her sudden jittery feeling, which seemed to be a mixture of fear and adrenaline.

Her friends silently watched her pace back and forth, before Celia raised her hand like she was in a classroom. 'Wait, it kinda sounds like he asked you not to leave. Is that right?'

Bonni jerked her head in a sharp nod and paced faster. Then Ava leapt up and grabbed her arm. 'Talk to us, Bonni. We've been friends for too long for you to keep anything from us now. We can help, we can listen, just don't bottle it up.'

Admitting defeat, Bonni patted Ava's hand and stopped pacing. 'Quinn wants me to miss my flight today and stay an extra night with him.'

'He does? What does that mean? It could be a good sign, right, like he wants to plan a future?' Celia looked at the others and held her palms out.

'We don't know.' Ava shrugged her shoulders. She tilted her

head toward Bonni. 'Bons, you have some decisions to make.' She wrapped her arms around Bonni. 'And you do know, that whatever you decide, we are here for you.'

Fredi came over and joined the hug. 'We're your squad, babe. We got your back no matter what you choose.'

Celia opened her arms and threw them around everybody, not that she could reach them all. 'Yes! Exactly. There's nothing more powerful than a strong tribe.'

'I know that.' Bonni smiled, feeling a little bit better after the reassurances from her friends. 'So what do you think I should do?'

'I think you should totally ditch the flight home and get a room. Stay the extra night and don't sweat it,' Celia said, taking down her hair and threading her fingers through it.

Ava was hot on her heels. 'Yes, you totally should. I know you scheduled an extra day for yourself, to recover from the jetlag before your next shift starts.'

'Oh, do-eeet!' Celia clutched the belt of the robe and bounced on her toes.

Bonni turned to Fredi. She was the barometer. The one who always made sense, and would tell you the logical thing to do, even if it wasn't what you wanted to hear. 'So?'

Fredi looked thoughtful. 'Listen, I've seen a lot of couples, and a lot of marriages, and I can tell if a couple will last.' She took Bonni's hands and pulled her around so she faced her, giving her a big smile. 'I can see it in you and Quinn. There's something there, so I think you need to take a leap of faith. Okay, you screwed up, ran out, said some apparently crappy things. Now go fight for him. Remember, you only live once.'

Ava gave Bonni a meaningful look, as Fredi's words eerily echoed Ava's from the other night. Was Quinn worth fighting for?

Everyone was silent. Bonni stared at Fredi. 'Wow, of everyone, you are the last one I'd expect to encourage me.'

Fredi nodded. 'But I am.'

Ava and Celia both chimed in. 'Me too.'

Bonni swelled up with emotion. It was the affirmation she needed to hear. 'Okay. Okay. I'm going to do it. I'll change my flight, get another room just in case, and then go wait for him. I just hope he can forgive me for what I said.'

'He loves you.' Fredi winked at her. 'Just say you're sorry and mean it. He'll forgive you.'

'I can't tell you what it means to me that I have you guys to lean on, that I can tell you everything and you won't judge.' Bonni looked at each of her friends in turn. Ava had tears in her eyes while Fredi lifted a shoulder, at her limit for dramatic emotional confessions, and Celia chewed her bottom lip.

'Of course no judgment! If you can't tell all your secrets to your best friends, who can you tell them to?' Ava said.

Fredi replied, 'Well, I don't know about that. I never told you guys about the time that I met this guy and—'

Celia suddenly screeched, 'Landon and I had sex!'

Bonni punched the air in triumph, her first happy emotion of the day. 'I KNEW IT!'

Chapter 25

Quinn kept his gaze glued to the pot. He knew that if he didn't get his shit together in a hurry, it could disappear into Dante's grubby fingers. Or one of the other players', for that matter. But Dante was his biggest threat and usually Quinn was on point. But not this time.

It was all he could do not to growl with frustration. He was off his game. He could feel it. And it showed. He'd played Dante before and knew his signals. Granted, he had a few new ones, but it wouldn't normally take Quinn this long to figure them out.

It's just that today is different. He had a distraction. A beautiful, sexy, wonderful and challenging distraction. And her name is Bonni.

Quinn mentally shook his head to try and dislodge the image of a naked Bonni from his brain. He looked at Dante and almost grimaced. The expression on his face right now, while blank to others, wasn't to Quinn. The wrinkle on the bridge of Dante's nose was him trying to bite back a smile. The slightly squinted eyes were also tell-tale. He was smug. He knew Quinn was off and he was capitalizing on it. Quinn wanted to smack that smug look right off his competitor's face. It wasn't the final round. They weren't the last two players. His opponents were whittling down, though, and soon it would be the final two. Damn straight he still wanted to win, but if he kept this attitude up it would be a snowball's chance in hell he'd make it to the final round.

He was having a very difficult time focusing. He wasn't overly concerned about the other players and kept his semi-focus on Dante. The prick. That, if anything, should spur Quinn on to kick his ass.

Somehow, after last night, things seem to have shifted for him. He glanced at the very stoic-faced dealer as he burned a card and dealt the river. Quinn stared without really seeing the cards. All he saw in his mind was Bonni.

The day had started so promisingly. He'd held her all night. And she had slept like a baby. In the morning, he had lain there, watching her sleep, feeling like the king of the world. Quinn stared blankly at his cards before they registered with him. The only thing he could see was the image of her fast asleep on the rumpled bed, looking so peaceful and lovely, and how cute she'd been, even if she had been drunk as a skunk. He'd been so sure that she'd be eager to stay, that they'd really be able to talk about building a future together. She'd lashed out at him. And he'd been stunned into speechlessness. Then she'd stormed out with those brutal words hanging in the air.

It had taken a moment for Quinn to gather his thoughts, and by the time he'd managed to unroot his feet from the ground and rush out the door after her, she was already gone, the elevator doors closing as he raced down the hall. There hadn't been time to follow her down and find her in the lobby, as much as he had wanted to. If he had, he would've been disqualified from this final round.

It wasn't like Quinn had asked her to do anything too major. All he wanted was for her to stay with him. An extra night. Why couldn't she just stay?

He separated a small stack of chips and shuffled them with his fingers. Contemplating his position and Bonni. The two were not mixing all that well together. He picked a chip and rolled it along his knuckles and stared at the cards.

He could feel Dante's excited energy. The other opponents weren't nearly so agitated. Landon had always said that Quinn had some kind of voodoo magic with cards and poker. Maybe he did. But right now, all he wanted was to end this game. Quinn flickered a glance at Dante, then back to his cards. He looked like he was getting smugger by the minute, so sure he had Quinn figured out. Insufferable ass.

Placing his cards face down, Quinn protected his hole cards by placing a chip on top. He hoped that it would unnerve Dante, because what Quinn was going to do next was risky.

'Keep playing that hand, buddy.' Dante's lightly accented voice had a mocking tone and Quinn knew he was taking a jab at his slow play. But he also noticed the quick glance Dante gave to the other players. Dante was feeling the pressure. Quinn held on to his poker face through sheer will. He didn't like to be told what to do; it was the whole reason he'd left home in the first place. He thought a little longer, then decided his next move was the right one. He checked.

There was a sinking feeling in Quinn's stomach as he realized that he hadn't asked Bonni what her plans were. He had just told her what he wanted her to do. And she'd bolted in a cloud of scathing words.

God. *He* was the insufferable ass.

For the first time ever, he was anxious to get a tournament wrapped up, eager to find Bonni. The words she'd said, while cutting him deep, were true. He watched Dante, and it was all he could do not to smile. He bet, and now Quinn acted.

'Raise. All in.' Quinn kept his voice monotone.

Dante's mouth thinned ever so slightly. He didn't even look at the others at the table. Now he was the one taking his time. There were murmurs from the crowd and Dante looked like he was going to levitate right out of his seat. He'd been nipping at Quinn's heels in the international rankings for years. The next move Dante made would be the end of this round as the others folded. *It's him or me going on to the final.* Quinn's head hadn't been in the game and he should have tossed his cards into the muck when his hole cards were first dealt. So now he had to draw on strategy and check-raise one seemed to be his best option.

Being rebellious only gets you so far, Quinn. At some point, you have to grow the fuck up.

He had wanted to be more than the man his father expected him to be. He wanted to be free to go his own way and make his own choices. Quinn continued to shuffle his chips. The clacking of them and the silence of Dante as he lifted the corner of his cards and put them down again didn't distract Quinn from staring at his cards. He realized, as he waited for Dante's move, that at some point defying society's norms had become a habit, not a choice.

It wasn't easy to find somebody you clicked with the way he and Bonni had. Or find that special someone you actually *wanted* to spend time with. Especially for him. Not that he was a love-'em-and-leave-'em kind of guy, but he was always ready to move on. No commitments. No professions of love. No promises to meet up again.

Until now. He wanted all of that with Bonni. Panic surged through him, and he willed Dante to hurry the fuck up and throw in his cards. Or, at the worst, raise him.

Dante moved a pile of his chips around and Quinn unconsciously held his breath. He was going to raise him. The check-raise wasn't going to work. Quinn was going to lose. He looked at the pot on the table. The winner's pot. And a lot of it his. He said a silent goodbye.

Quinn had a powerful realization. The clarity that hit him right now tilted his world. If he lost, he wouldn't care. He already had money. Boatloads of it. But if he lost Bonni . . . well, that couldn't happen. His heart hurt, it was pounding so fast. Normally, his adrenaline rush came from the game and from winning. But now it came from the panic of potentially losing Bonni. He was done. This was it. His last tournament. Once it was over, then he'd go after her.

He looked around, hoping to see her in the audience. That would mean she'd decided to stay. But she wasn't.

He knew what he needed to do. One last tournament. Now, he wanted to win. Wanted his strategy to work. Go out on top, crushing Dante like a bug. And then go after her.

Winning Bonni back would be the only victory that mattered.

He looked at Dante, square on, giving him no tells. And when Dante stared back at him he thinned his lips and Quinn felt the hate coming off him in waves.

Dante tossed in his cards. He folded. Quinn had won on a bluff. All that was left was the final game.

And going after Bonni.

Chapter 26

Bonni stepped off the elevator into the crush of the crowd. She had to get to the front desk and find a room for tonight. She'd already switched her flight. Driven by a new determination, she pushed her way through the crowd.

Damn! You would think that, since Vegas never sleeps, the lobby would be deserted this early in the morning, but she was astounded at the number of people who were gambling at all hours of the day. She could see a big line at the front desk and her heart dropped. *I need a room!*

'Bonni.' She halted when she heard her name, and turned. Landon approached.

'Hi.' She didn't really know what to say to him. They'd had an enjoyable conversation at the patisserie, but Quinn had been there to smooth over the rough spots, and she hadn't really spoken to Landon since then. They'd not said more than a few words the other night in the bar before she'd left with Quinn. Things were even more awkward now that she knew Landon was equally as good as Quinn at certain things. *Thanks a lot, Celia!*

'How are you? Enjoying Vegas?' The gleam in his eye indicated to her that he was referring to a whole lot more than just gambling.

'Sure. You?' She wasn't about to say too much. She had no idea if Quinn had told him about last night. When the parting words she had said to Quinn rang in her ears, she inwardly cringed. Glancing over Landon's shoulder, she chewed her lip, desperate to get in the line.

'Always. You never know what will happen in Vegas. Like, for example, you and Quinn meeting up.'

She narrowed her eyes and assessed him. What was he trying to say? Her cop side started awakening from its vacation slumber. 'I'm glad I met Quinn. He's a very special man.'

Landon nodded. 'I agree. He's my brother, after all.' He shot her a big smile. 'He's the sensitive one.'

'And you are . . . ?'

He raised a shoulder. 'The ruthless one.'

She flashbacked to the veiled bedtime story Quinn had shared. Bonni looked up at Landon. 'You don't seem all that ruthless to me. Nosey, maybe, but not ruthless.'

He laughed. 'I like your candor. There's no real need to be ruthless here. I consider myself on a quick vacation. But the boardroom is a different game.'

'And Quinn, he's not in the boardroom?' Bonni asked the leading question and waited to hear his answer.

'No, no. I've tried for years to bring him in, but he's the independent one. Out to face the world and make a name for himself. But I know he's considering coming back.'

Bonni glanced at the floor. She hadn't really had a chance to let the end of Quinn's story sink in. *Doing something that he's never wanted to do in order to be with his lady.* She repeated her words from last night, 'He should be able to be who he wants to be.'

Raising her head, she gave Landon a fierce look. 'You're just going to have to fire him if he decides to come back.'

Landon pressed his lips together and crossed his arms. 'Well, now, don't you sound just like him. So very protective.' They maintained eye contact for an intense couple of seconds before he looked away. 'So, will you be seeing each other after Vegas?'

'If there's anything I can do about it, then yes. I love him for who he is. Not who everyone wants him to be.' Bonni heard her voice break and swallowed, determined not to lose it in the hotel lobby.

'It won't be easy,' Landon warned. 'It's not your typical nine-to-five job. He goes to a lot of different places, and some of them are terrifying to think about. With the time differences, sometimes it'll be days before you hear from him, and even then, his response could be just a quick email. And the money—'

Bonni interrupted angrily. 'I don't care about the money! And, yes, staying at home while he leaves me behind will be difficult, but to be with him, it would all be worth it.'

Landon regarded her thoughtfully. 'I believe you mean that.'

'I do mean it. Look, I'm not claiming this was an easy decision to make, especially since we haven't known each other long, but it's the right one. What Quinn and I have is worth exploring.'

Landon looked down to adjust the sleeves of his buttoned-down shirt and then said, 'So stop talking to me and go find him.'

'I have to book my room and then get my bags to concierge first. We were supposed to check out today.' Bonni tried to keep panic from setting in.

Landon shook his head. 'I doubt you'll have a problem finding a place to sleep tonight, not if my brother has anything to say about it, but I'll take care of everything.' He leaned down and brushed a kiss over her cheek. 'I have a limo waiting at the valet. Go to him.'

Impulsively, Bonni threw her arms around him for a hug. She felt him startle, before he tentatively placed an arm around her shoulder to hug her back. Stepping back, she looked up and said, 'Thank you. I really appreciate what you're doing for me and Quinn. But, Landon, if you hurt Celia, I will find a way to add you to the no-fly list. I know people.'

Bonni pivoted on her heel and ran to the valet, hearing a crack of laughter behind her. Once in the limo, she texted her friends, asking them to throw all her stuff into her suitcase and that Landon would be stopping by to collect it.

Now that she was finally on her way to Quinn, she felt she could take a moment to breathe. She looked out the car window and last night's bedtime story again came back in a rush. One line stood out in vivid clarity.

A girl who, in a very short space of time, turned his world upside down.

He'd been talking about *her*.

Could he love her too?

Chapter 27

Quinn could taste victory. No way was he going to smile at the wrong time or give any indication of the cards that were in his hand. The TV cameras were cruising around their table. This final round was televised. He kept his attention in front and stared down at the chips, at the pot, glanced once at his cards and slid them over the viewer for the audience to see. He put them in front of him and placed his hands palm down on the table.

Quinn tuned out the large crowd. From under the shadow of his baseball cap and behind his mirrored aviators, he swiveled his gaze around the table. Scrutinizing his opponents, watching for a twitch here or a nervous touch to the face there. He knew these players and their idiosyncrasies. He'd crushed them before in other tournaments.

They knew it, and he knew it. The floor was hushed, and the only sound was the players shuffling their chips. He closed his eyes and tuned out all the sounds around him. It was like a collective sigh sucked the air out of the room.

He needed a king to complete his flush. His hand was good, a winning hand, but it all came down to the river. He drew in a quiet breath and held it. Waiting for the turn of the card.

The dealer played the last one and it was all Quinn could do not to leap from his chair with the roar. The card he needed showed its pretty face to him. He quickly looked at the other players from behind his sunglasses, trying to catch any expression they might reveal on their faces.

It didn't matter. Quinn had to go all in now. For two reasons. One, because he had an excellent hand and two, because this was his last game. It was go big or go home. After the last round of betting, the pot was the biggest he'd ever played for. It was over $2 million. The others would have to ante up or fold. They all matched his bet and called. Quinn watched the cards and refused to let nerves play with him.

It was time for the showdown. Each player preceding him put their cards face up, and he knew he had it. When he laid his cards, the place erupted. He had won. The thrill of the win spiked an adrenaline rush. And he knew this was another reason he played. He enjoyed the excitement that came from playing poker. The satisfaction of winning, beating the cards and his opponents.

Only, it would be his last time.

He stood up and shook everyone's hand.

A crowd surrounded him. He wasn't able to avoid them, and it frustrated the hell out of Quinn.

'Great game,' one opponent said to him. 'Are you doing the Caribbean challenge?'

They shook hands, and Quinn knew he was distracted. His focus had completely veered from poker to Bonni. But at the question about the Caribbean Challenge, he was pulled up short. Quinn paused and realized how easy it was to answer the question. He smiled and shook his head. 'No, not this year. Good luck to you.'

'Thanks, man.'

He gritted his teeth, knowing that he couldn't leave yet. The sponsors needed to do their thing. He had to say something, and the Royal Flush Girls would be coming out to help celebrate. There'd be interviews, television spots, promo ops . . . and all Quinn wanted to do was get the hell out of here. But he was a professional. And it was expected.

The crowd grew, and he was swarmed. But it didn't stop him from keeping a hawk eye on the crowd for Bonni.

Then he saw her shiny dark hair like a beacon. She pushed her way through the throng toward him. He felt the smile crack wide on his face. She saw him, and their gazes locked over the distance. Bonni pointed to the lounge area and then at herself. He nodded and watched her make her way to the bar.

Suddenly, Quinn felt ecstatic. The win paled in comparison to seeing Bonni here. That meant she had stayed, and was willing to miss her flight so they could talk. They now had some precious time to discuss their situation. How they would make it work and what was to come. He had the urge to run over, snatch her up and whisk her away to places unknown so nothing could take her away from him.

He kept glancing over at her. She was watching him, and they smiled at each other. He finished up the interview and, finally, his obligations were over. He slipped away from the hubbub.

Bonni was facing the bar, holding a glass of water. Quinn saw a couple of men gathered around her. One was being a particular pain to Bonni. She turned to him and said something, and the expression on her face left no room for interpretation. She was mad. An answering anger flared inside Quinn. The douchebag was all over his woman.

Logically, he knew that Bonni was a cop and could take care of herself. Still, he found himself charging over there like the bear he'd been nicknamed after in college. Quinn pulled up when he saw Bonni whirl around and grab the guy's hand which had just been on her ass. Within seconds, he was twisted up like a pretzel and down on one knee in front of her. Quinn watched her handle the man. People beside her were startled and Security appeared out of nowhere to escort the man away somewhere to, presumably, lick his wounds.

'Holy shit. That was impressive.'

And it was then he realized there was so much more to her than he'd unraveled these last couple of days. She was the most fascinating woman he'd ever met, and one that had crept into his heart. More intriguing and beguiling than any other woman he'd ever known. Her feistiness is what had caught his attention that first night. Her zest for life was a breath of fresh air, and her willingness to experience new things. Like stepping outside her comfort zone, as she proved in his room up against the window. Quinn's chest tightened and his desire for her roared back to the surface. He'd kept it dampened all day, and it threatened to unleash itself. And her self-defense techniques were a huge turn-on. He swallowed and fisted his hands.

Quinn wove between the people milling around, not taking his eyes off her. She was magnificent in her outrage. She raised her hands, arched her back and ran her fingers through her hair, shaking it out. She watched the man get carted away and Quinn drew in a breath. Her cheeks were flushed and her eyes flashing. Quinn was turned on and he needed to get back under control or it would be evident to anyone that cared to look below his belt.

Bonni turned, and her gaze fell on him. The fury on her face melted into joy. Her smile beckoned him and the ire in her eyes turned to happiness. He felt like he'd been punched in the gut and it was all he could do to breathe. She'd been so angry at him this morning and he was relieved to see that she wasn't any longer.

'Quinn!' She ran to him and he scooped her up. She hooked a leg around him and wrapped her arms around his neck. For the first time, he truly understood her strength, independence and power. It captivated him even more.

'What are you doing, trying to pick fights with douchebags?'

'Right? That guy just wouldn't take no for an answer.'

'Well, you surely showed him the consequences, no doubt about that.' He let her slide down his body, in a move that tortured them both, then took her hand and pulled her close.

Bonni's smile faded and she looked up at him through her eyelashes. 'Quinn, about this morning—'

Another fan came over to congratulate Quinn and, in the distance, he could see a rep from one of his sponsors searching the crowds. 'Hold that thought, Temptress. Let's go get a private table before we get interrupted again.'

She looked up at him and he swooped in for another kiss, unable to resist her.

'I'll go anywhere you want me to, Quinn.'

He may have just won millions of dollars, but it was in this precise moment that Quinn felt like the luckiest man alive.

Chapter 28

A sizeable tip to the maître d' got them a secluded table in the American New Wave restaurant on the top floor of the hotel. It was a nice place, and Quinn was wearing his usual poker outfit, looking dashingly handsome, while Bonni wore a dress that showcased her fantastic legs. Her hair, as always, swung in a glossy dark curtain around her neck. He noticed she had on the same killer shoes she'd worn the night they met. After accepting the tip, the man hadn't made a peep, just shown them to the table, and now Quinn was looking at her like she was the most beautiful woman in the world.

The maître d' held the chair for Bonni, and she sat, then he took the napkin and laid it across her lap, before assisting her in pushing the chair back in. The table was next to a large picture window, overlooking the Strip. Bonni turned to look at the view while Quinn sat. She imagined that the view must be truly impressive at night. 'Vegas really is pretty, isn't it?'

'It is. It can either love you or hate you. And I think, this trip, it loves me.'

Bonni rapped her knuckles against the table. 'Touch wood. You don't want to jinx anything.'

'I've already won.' He smiled across at her, and she felt a warm, languid feeling curl in her belly.

'It can't hurt, can it? You can never have too much luck.'

'Being here with you, Temptress, I have all the luck I need.' Bonni felt her cheeks flush and he gave her a wicked grin. She just knew he was thinking about their last discussion about her blushes. He opened his mouth but, before he could say something completely inappropriate, the waiter came over with the wine list.

'I think I'm going to have a glass of ice wine. Would you like some?' Quinn handed the list back to the waiter.

'Canadian ice wine?' Bonni asked, a little surprised he would know Canadian ice wine.

'Of course, it's the best. I've wine-toured the Niagara Region. Very interesting how the vineyards began there.'

While the waiter fetched their wine, they looked at the menu. When he returned, Quinn said, 'I think my lovely companion and I will start with—'

Bonni cleared her throat, and Quinn smoothly changed course. 'What I mean to say is that I will start with Caesar salad and extra croutons and then have the rack of lamb.'

Hiding her smile behind her menu, Bonni advised the waiter that she would have the same as Quinn. After the man left, Quinn gave her a sheepish grin. 'Sorry. Habit.'

Bonni leaned over the table and reached for his hand. 'One more thing you need to learn about me. I don't mind chivalrous gentlemen, and it's rather romantic too. But, food, I don't like nuts, remember.' She winked. 'So I was worried you might misfire on the order.'

Quinn laughed, and a few heads turned in their direction.

Bonni realized just how happy she was. 'These last few days have been wonderful. Meeting you was such . . . I don't even know how to describe it! There are so many reasons I've enjoyed being with you. Meeting you was the last thing I ever expected to happen on this trip when I came here with my friends.'

'I told you the other night, you are the most fantastic surprise that could've ever happened to me.' He smiled. and she felt the warmth of his sincerity.

'So unexpected. Delightfully unexpected.' Bonni looked out the window again, at Las Vegas below, glinting in the sunlight. 'Are we shining bright just like the casino lights do? And once we leave, immerse ourselves back into our everyday life, will the light in our relationship fade? Just like the bright lights of Vegas will dim in our memory over time.'

'If there's anything I've learned, you cannot predict tomorrow. And why all it's about building memories. Haven't we already talked about this?' Quinn squeezed her hand before reaching for his glass and taking a sip of his wine. She admired the line of his throat as he swallowed.

Bonni agreed. 'You're right. You've made me understand how important it is to live in the present. In my line of work, I'm always digging into the past to work out what's happened and hopefully stop something bad from happening in the future. That includes putting my own life on the line sometimes.'

'That is something,' Quinn said in a low voice, curling his fingers around her wrist before continuing, 'that I don't like the thought of one little bit.' Bonni loved the feel of his touch. He gave her goosebumps, and heat flared up her arm, spreading through her body in a delicious wave.

'It comes with the territory, I'm afraid.' She turned her hand over so she could lace her fingers with his.

'I don't like the idea of a world without you in it. As it was, I didn't expect to see you at the tournament. I thought you'd be long gone by now.' He pressed a kiss to her hand and lowered his voice. 'Especially the way you left this morning.'

Bonni felt a rush of shame at the memory of how she'd thrown the way he'd opened up to her back in his face. 'I'm sorry about what I said this morning. The way you just assumed I have no problem changing my flight, and when you said you change your travel plans all the time, I got angry and I got scared, and I lashed out. I'm so sorry, Quinn.'

He reached out with his free hand to cup her cheek. 'It's okay. I wanted you to stay so badly, I didn't let myself think about what obligations were waiting for you back home. And, besides, you had a point.'

'No! No, I didn't. I don't want you to change. It's why I stayed. I just couldn't bring myself to go, to leave you behind. So I did a lot of thinking. I want to come with you. I want to see the world as you see the world. I want to travel and explore with you. Be spontaneous.' She rushed her words, unable to keep them steady and calm. It was important for her to blurt it all out as quickly as possible. She needed him to know, to understand.

The look of joy on his face was her answer. 'I'm stunned. Bonni, the fact that you would do this for me means so much. But you don't have to do this—'

He fell silent as the waiter brought their starter. The food looked amazing, but her attention was solely focused on Quinn. She had to keep talking so he would know how serious she was about this.

'The thing is, I called earlier today and I could only get another two weeks of leave right now. And I have to go back after that to work out my final notice. They may not be too happy with me but, as you know, I was planning on moving to Virginia soon anyway.'

Tossing his napkin on the table, Quinn left his seat so he could kneel next to her. He placed his hands on either side of her face and tilted it so they could look into each other's eyes. 'Bonni, I'm out.'

'Out?' She wasn't quite sure what he was referring to.

He nodded. 'Yes. I'm out. Off the circuit. I decided to take the job with Bryant Enterprises. I'll have to do a little traveling, visit the main headquarters from time to time, but I can basically call work from anywhere. And you won't ever have to worry about expenses for your dad or moving to Virginia. We will never have any money issues.'

Bonni clutched his wrists and tried to shake her head. 'Quinn, no, you can't. You don't have to do this, not for me.'

His fingers stroked her temples. 'Darling, I'm not doing it just for you. I'm doing it for my brother, who needs me around to help him get the stick out of his ass and to help with the family. I'm doing it for myself. I've been running from my father's expectations for so long, I never stopped to demand more from myself. I've proven I can be a success away from my family and now it's time to see what else I can do. And I'm doing it for us. Because I want to wake up with you every morning and go to sleep with you every night. I want to be there when you go see your father and I want to pick you up from the bar when your friends come to visit and I want be the person who stays by your side, no matter what. I love you, Bonni.'

It was the most romantic thing Bonni had ever heard. It felt like a dream come true. Tears sprang to her eyes. 'Quinn, oh, wow. I'm . . . I don't know what to say.'

'There's nothing to say, except yes. Yes, we'll give it a try and yes, you'll come with me, wherever, for the next two weeks.'

'Yes, yes! I love you too!' Bonni threw her arms around his neck, nearly causing the two of them to topple over. He pulled her up into a huge bear hug, rocking them a little from side to side.

'You have made me the happiest man.' He whispered the words into her ear, sending a flurry of shivers over her skin.

She looked up at him and wasn't the least bit ashamed when the tears started trickling down her face.

'Oh, come now, there's no need for tears.' Quinn leaned forward and, with his free hand, swept his thumb under her eyes.

Suddenly, Bonni registered the sound of applause and realized the other diners had mistaken Quinn's offer to change his life for her as a proposal. Bonni did what she could to compose herself, but the raw emotion he made her feel was overwhelming. He'd ripped her open, and bared her inner soul, but in a way that made her realize just how closed off she'd kept herself. How was that living?

'I don't remember the last time I've been this overcome.' She turned her face away.

'Don't look away from me.' Quinn put his fingers under her chin and gently turned her back to him.

'Oh,' she said, and sniffed. 'I'm not turning away from you, Quinn, I just don't want anybody else to see me cry.'

'The only ones here that matter are me and you.'

That was when the waiter came over with a complimentary bottle of champagne and the best wishes of the management. They had mistaken her celebration as acceptance of Quinn's wedding proposal. The waiter discreetly slipped her an extra napkin then vanished as quickly as he'd come. Looking at the champagne, she had to laugh, because it really had been that kind of trip.

Quinn kissed her forehead then helped her sit back in her chair. Suddenly hungry, they both devoured their appetizers and then their entrees. They decided against dessert, feeling the need to bask a little longer in the glow of their romance.

He stood and held out his hand for her, and didn't let it go as they rode down in the elevator. Strolling down the Strip, Quinn pointed out little things that he thought she might find interesting. They stopped at the Hershey store and she bought Quinn a small bag of Hershey's caramel kisses for their next breakfast in bed. Not to be outdone, he popped into the Walgreens and came out with several king-sized bags of Skittles. Those, he informed her, would be for dessert. And he wasn't going to need a plate.

She shivered at the heat in his gaze and they decided it was time to head back to pick up the limo.

'A crowd's gathering at the fountains. It must be show time.' Bonni dragged Quinn over to a small, empty spot next to the railing.

'Have you seen them before?' He stood behind her and wrapped his arms around her waist. Bonni snuggled back into him and leaned against his chest. She rested her hands on his forearms.

'When we were here years ago, I think we stopped to watch them, or were walking by. But I barely remember.'

'Oh?' he said, leaning down to nip at her neck.

Bonni tilted her head back so she could look at him. He gazed down at her with a mischievous grin. This was the Quinn she had fallen for. She said, in a very serious voice, 'Honestly,

I'm having a hard time remembering my life before you were in it.'

Quinn's blue eyes went molten and she reached up to pull his head down for a kiss. When their lips met, and his tongue sought hers, she melted into him. Thank God he held her, because the passion he poured into their kiss compounded the emotion that was rioting through her body and made her knees tremble. One hand was behind his head and the other clutching his arm. But she needn't have worried, as he held her with a strength that made her able to forget her natural instinct to be in control.

He lifted away from her, leaving her gasping for air and every nerve alight with a fire only he was able to stoke so wildly. He didn't have a poker face now. She could read him; it was like he'd opened himself and let his emotions tumble out.

He drew in a breath. 'Woman, I don't know what I will do with you.'

'I was thinking the same thing.'

Quinn cleared his throat. 'And you're lucky we're in public right now.'

Feeling sassy, she replied, 'If I wasn't a cop, I don't know if being in public would be a deterrent.'

He practically purred, 'Now that sounds like a challenge. It's certainly not a no.'

'I refuse to answer on the basis it may incriminate me.' Bonni liked the lighter, more playful banter between them.

Quinn let out a bark of laughter. Music began, coming from carefully concealed speakers in the bushes and trees that ringed the fountains. They fell silent when the first spray of water shot in a stunning arc from a pool. It was breathtaking how beautiful the display was. The water danced to the music and Bonni was spellbound.

'No matter how many times I see the fountains, I'm still impressed with them.' Quinn rested his chin on the top of her head.

'It definitely is something to be impressed about.'

The show wound up and the crowd dispersed. Quinn led Bonni into the shuffle of people and they were carried along the sidewalk toward the hotel.

'I don't want this to end.' Bonni wrapped her arm around his waist and tucked her face into his shoulder, warm in the curve of his arm that held her so tight. Before they reached the front of the hotel she pulled him to a stop. He raised an eyebrow in curiosity.

'This has been absolutely amazing. A dream come true. When I tell Ava about this, she is just going to swoon. But, Quinn . . . I need to ask one more time. Are you sure about this? You're talking about changing your entire life for me, and we've practically just met.'

Quinn sighed and then looked around before dragging Bonni around the corner. The architecture of the building created small secluded alcoves and he pushed her into one, pressing her against the stone, warm from the Vegas sunshine. With his arms around her, she was surrounded by his presence, feeling both comforted and oh so safe. He kissed her again, one that started off sweet before rapidly evolving into something passionate and wild.

He raised his head, just enough so that they were barely touching, and she was bracing herself against his arms because her knees were so weak.

'Ask me,' Quinn said.

'What?' Bonni was breathless again, and all she wanted to do was close the gap between their lips.

'You know what,' Quinn replied, dropping an oh-too-short kiss against her mouth. 'Ask me.'

It took a few moments for her brain to kick into gear, and then Bonni smiled. It was a smile so huge she could feel her cheeks stretching to their limit.

'Still in?' she asked.

'All in,' he corrected. 'Always.'

Chapter 29

Bonni had left Landon's limo with the Bellagio's valet and, once the fountain show was over, they had the driver bring the car around. As soon as the luxury vehicle pulled up to the stand, Quinn bundled her inside. He pressed the speaker to the driver and instructed, 'Take a long way back to the Gladiators, please.' Bonni giggled as Quinn raised the privacy glass.

'Have you ever seen the old classic movie *No Way Out*?' Quinn asked her.

'No, can't say that I have.'

'Well, I think we're going to recreate the limo scene.'

'Oh, that sounds exciting. Can the driver see us?' she asked.

Quinn pulled Bonni on to his lap and pushed her skirt up around her hips. 'No, he can't see us through the darkened glass. I wouldn't start this if I thought he could. I don't share.'

'Good.' She let out a little surprised yelp when Quinn grabbed her ass fiercely and yanked her toward him. His erection was hard, insistent, and the only way to relieve the ache between her thighs. 'Make love to me, Quinn.'

'I plan to, darling, today and many days to come.'

Bonni settled on his thighs, gazing down at him through the fall of her hair. She rested her palms on his shoulders, then quickly pulled his shirt over his head. She drew in a ragged breath at the sight of him.

'To think we could have gone down the other path, where we never would have this again,' Bonni whispered, and drew her nails lightly over his skin. His powerful body trembled under her delicate touch.

Quinn reached up and placed his hands on her thighs, sliding them up over her hips, taking the hem of her dress with them. He curled his fingers around the filmy material of her panties and quickly pulled, ripping them off her.

'Oh my God.' She closed her eyes and arched her back, loving these wild emotions he invoked in her.

'You are the most beautiful woman.'

He continued the trek of his hand up her rib cage.

'Arms up.'

She did as he demanded, her fingers touching the roof of the limo. He removed her dress. She watched him, the expression on his face so intense and concentrated. Bonni shivered when he cupped her breasts, brushing his thumbs over her nipples.

'Oh, Quinn,' Bonni moaned, and tipped her head back. Her nipples hardened into sensitive peaks under the warmth of his palms, she arched, her back pressing deeper into him. She wanted so much more than just his thumbs exciting her. She wanted all of him, and she curled her fingers around his wrists.

They stared into each other's eyes, moving seductively in tune with each other, and the rock of the limo increased their cadence. He still wore his jeans, and her pussy rubbed deliciously against the rough fabric. Bonni licked her lips then pulled her lower one between her teeth to keep from moaning out loud.

'I could watch you like this for ever.' The tightness of his voice told her he was as turned on as she was. Bonni slid off him until she was kneeling on the limo floor. She leaned over him, low enough to plant a kiss on his chest, brush her lips softly over his nipples. He hissed and jolted when she nipped at them. Her hair, a glossy curtain, swept over his skin.

'You can, we can. For ever. I'm so glad we've crossed our hurdle.' Sitting back, Quinn undid his jeans and lifted his hips so she could pull them down. She took his cock in her hand, squeezing and stroking gently. She watched him, and what her touch did to him. She wrapped her fingers around his thickness, and caressed his hard length. The groans he gave spurred her on. Bending over, she placed her mouth at the tip of him, both of her hands firm and tight on his penis. Quinn's hands clustered in her hair, and he held his breath as she opened her lips, swirling her tongue around the sensitive glans and taking him deep into her mouth.

The desire to explore him more thoroughly than she had the previous times and the reality that they were beginning something beautiful together intensified her desire. Bonni closed her eyes, lost herself in the moment and gave pleasure to Quinn. She was creating memories the two of them would cherish.

Keeping him in her mouth, she ran her hands up to his chest, her fingertips mapping and memorizing the hard planes and ridges of his belly as she explored lower, to his hips, while she played and excited him with her mouth. Quinn's groans and the grip of his fingers in her hair thrilled her.

'Enough, Temptress, you're too good at that.' He gently lifted her head.

Quinn put his hands under her arms and pulled her higher on him until she was straddling him again. Bonni reached for her purse.

'This time, I'm the prepared one.' She smiled and pulled a package from her purse.

She rose on her knees, reaching between them to grasp his cock, sheathed him, then guided him into her.

They both moaned as she lowered herself down, fully receiving him, and began to rock her hips. He placed one hand on her shoulder and his other between them, his fingers finding her clitoris. Her body jolted under his swirling fingers. She grasped her breasts, holding them, as she rode him.

Eyes closed, and shifting into pure sensation, she tumbled into a sensory world. Feeling, hearing their sexual sounds. She licked her lips and tasted Quinn on them. Gasping for breath, Bonni's cadence increased until she was on the brink. The limo went over a bump in the road and she let out a cry when her orgasm teased her. She collapsed on Quinn, his hand still between them and he increased the pressure of his fingers.

Her body had a mind of its own, she had no control, and being with Quinn was the only place she needed to be. Wanted to be. She rode him harder, more frantically, until her orgasm powered through her. She held her breath and fell over him, her hands on his shoulders meeting the upward thrust of his hips. He growled deep in his chest and his fingers were relentless on her now super-sensitive flesh until another, deeper orgasm grew inside her.

She moaned, a low sound that had the characteristics of a primal being.

'Oh, you're making me come apart again.' Her face was tucked into the curve at the base of his neck and he wrapped his free arm around her shoulders, holding her tight to his chest.

Her second climax shattered through her, and she was carried into another dimension.

'Oh, Quinn.' Her was voice raspy and low.

She pressed her lips to the hollow at the base of his throat and gently sucked. The rhythm of his vein throbbed, matching the thump of her heart.

'We – are . . .' Quinn didn't finish the sentence. He turned her head until he could claim her mouth. He kissed her deep, with a control that was both exciting and full of anticipation. Bonni slid her tongue into his mouth, seeking. Tasting. Remembering. She vowed never to forget this moment.

Quinn moaned into her and powered his hips. She tightened herself around him, as he wrapped her in his powerful arms, their kiss unbroken. A low growl built in him, and then he stiffened, was still and collapsed back on the limo seat, with her draped over his chest.

His breathing was ragged and Bonni swept her hand through his hair. Glancing up, she looked at him as he caught his breath. He turned, she smiled at his eyes, half closed, and he kissed her. A soft, loving and promising kiss.

'Can anything top that?' Bonni murmured against his lips.

'I doubt it.' He pressed a kiss to the corner of her mouth.

The spent a few precious moments in each other's embrace as their bodies came down from the passionate high.

Everything was going to be okay. They were going to figure it out.

Bonni fixed her dress while Quinn got his clothes organized. He opened the hideaway bar. 'Anything to drink?'

'Uhm, well, is there champagne? After all, I do believe we have something to celebrate.'

'As a matter of fact, there is a chilled bottle just waiting to be opened.'

'Excellent.' Bonni watched him handle the bottle the way he had the other night and pour them each a glass.

'To us.' He held his glass out and she touched the crystal flute to his.

'Mmm, I seem to be developing a taste for the bubbly,' Bonni said, after she'd had a decent sip. 'I wonder how often this sort of thing happens in Vegas?'

'What, the champagne?'

'No silly, the sex. What we did . . . in the limo.' Heat rushed over her cheeks and she couldn't believe she was blushing.

'I'm pretty sure it happens much more often than you could imagine.' Quinn pressed a button and the sunroof opened.

Sun streamed in and warmed her. Bonni sat back and enjoyed the heat on her face. She felt like she hadn't been outside in ages. Everything always seemed so indoorsy in Vegas. Then she jumped up and tried to stand.

'Oh, awesome. I've always wanted to do this too.'

Bonni gripped Quinn's knees and moved one hand up to the roof. She slowly stood up through the open window. Quinn's strong hands held her thighs as the limo drove down Las Vegas Boulevard with her popped up out of the roof. The combination of his fingers, the wind whipping her hair and the sun beating down on her face made her unbelievably happy. She let out a whoop, feeling like she had the world on fire.

'Get back down in here, Bonni,' Quinn demanded.

'Just a few more minutes. This is glorious!' she shouted.

'You do know that you can get into a lot of trouble for not having your seatbelt on,' Quinn informed her.

She laughed and called back down through the window, 'You're preaching to the choir, my man.'

'Bonni, if you don't get back in now, I'm going to pull you down. I don't need you jettisoning out the window if there's an accident.'

She flopped on to the seat beside him, so deliriously happy. 'I don't think this day could've gotten any better.'

With the sun lighting up the interior of the limo, Bonni

raised her hand to shield her eyes. Quinn grabbed it and stared down at her. Feeling slightly self-conscious, she asked, 'What is it?'

Pressing a kiss against her palm, he replied, 'I knew your eyes would be glorious in the sunlight. I can't wait to see what else I discover about you.'

Feeling so tender, she snuggled close to him. 'Likewise. And now, we have all the time in the world to make those discoveries together.'

Chapter 30

When the limo arrived at the valet stand at the Gladiators, Quinn got out first. He stood beside it, and glanced around. The hustle in the valet area told him the hotel was hopping. There were the usual mix of designer dresses and tourist wear, as the familiar noise of Vegas filled the air. Quinn leaned down and reached his hand into the car for Bonni.

She placed hers in his and he was mesmerized when one long leg emerged from the car. It didn't matter how many times he looked at her, naked, or clothed, his body reacted with a power that took his breath away. Even though they'd just had sex in the limo, the sight of her shapely leg was enough to bring him to his knees.

'Now that's a sight I could see every day,' he told her.

'What is?' Her voice, low and sultry, came from the darkened interior of the car.

'Your leg.' He watched as she stepped out, her hair, dark, glossy and windblown from standing out of the sunroof. It was so dark, it almost shone blue under the lights. Her face was still flushed from her orgasms. It was all he could do not to throw her over his shoulder and whisk her up to his room. 'And I know you're not wearing any panties, Temptress.'

She stood tall next to him and gave him a seductive sideways glance. 'Well, that, my bear, is all your doing.'

He chuckled and took her hand. 'All the better for when we get up to my room.' He kissed her cheek. 'Mind the curb.' He guided her over the cobblestone walk.

She held his hand tightly as she stepped up to the walkway and turned to wait for him. Quinn leaned down and spoke to the driver.

They walked into the hotel and Quinn was positive Bonni had no idea of the looks she was getting. He was proud to have her on his arm. Proud that this strong and independent woman had chosen him. He looked down at her and his chest swelled. She was his. The future was theirs for the taking.

'Oh, Quinn, look.' She pointed. 'There must be a toga party going on.' She looked up at him. 'I've always wanted to dress up in a toga.'

'What, no wild college toga parties? All the hijinks I'm sure you and your friends got into, and not a single toga party?'

She laughed and shook her head. 'Nope. Fredi always said being wrapped in a bed sheet was not acceptable party attire.'

'Well, we can create our own toga party up in my room and you can model the latest toga fashion for me.' He put his hand on her shoulder and squeezed gently.

'Now, that is definitely a promise I will make you keep. Maybe we can play Greek God and Peasant Girl?' Bonni said saucily, and Quinn groaned, shifting slightly behind her.

She giggled and then said, 'You know, I think I'd like to come back to Vegas again one day.'

Bonni looked up at him, and he loved the expression in her eyes. It held promise of a future.

'Maybe we could come back together and, you never know, we could wind up at one of those little wedding chapels.' He was half joking when he said it, but Landon had been right when he said that Quinn knew how to read people. Bonni was the one.

'Elope? You and I?' Bonni smiled and her eyes danced, before she burst out laughing. 'Do you really think my friends would be satisfied with a quickie elopement? And Fredi will totally want to design my wedding dress.'

The image of Bonni wearing a wedding gown and walking down the aisle to him, it struck him with the force of a bullet. For the last decade of his life he had avoided anything remotely traditional and dodged any attempt at being tied down. Now, with Bonni, he couldn't imagine his future any other way.

'Just as long as what happens in Vegas doesn't stay in Vegas.' He grabbed her and hugged her tight.

'I like the sound of that.'

'So do I.' Never did he ever think he'd be the one to settle down. But, obviously, he'd met the woman who had changed all that.

He ran his thumb down her neck and across her shoulder. A delicate shiver rippled through her. He couldn't take his eyes off her. What he wanted most in this moment was to get her up to his room and make love to her, to celebrate the fact that she was his and he was hers. As they rounded into the lobby, he heard loud applause and celebratory whoops.

'What the hell?' He looked over and saw Ava, Fredi, Celia and Landon in the lobby next to the bar. 'This is totally going to waylay our plans to get up to my room. You had to text them to tell them we were coming back here, didn't you?'

While Quinn was slightly frustrated that their lovemaking would be delayed, he was primarily amused, especially after one passer-by nearly took a header when he was distracted by Ava jumping up and down. 'They're creating a spectacle.'

Bonni laughed and tugged Quinn in the direction of her friends and his brother.

'I know, but who cares? Nobody will remember this after today. Only those who matter to us. And those people are right over there, waiting for us.'

Quinn looked at them and realized she was right. With Bonni came the sisters of her heart, and he was looking forward to being able to spend more time with his brother. 'Well, they are certainly excited.'

She looked up at him. 'Love me, love my friends.'

'Oh, I do. Love you, that is.'

Quinn swept her up in his arms and kissed her. Right there in the middle of the bustling Gladiators lobby, among the throng of guests and in front of the four people that mattered in their lives.

Quinn didn't want to let her go but, reluctantly, he put her back on her feet. Bonni's head was thrown back and she was laughing. Her eyes were shining with love for him, and the cheers from her friends and his brother broke through his passion for this wonderful woman in his arms.

Bonni turned and pulled him over to the group waiting for them. Then she shouted out at the top of her lungs. 'Don't worry, ladies, he's not staying in Vegas!'

And he wouldn't have it any other way.

WORKING GIRL

A sexy seven-day job interview.
Seven irresistible interviewers.
Who will she choose at the end of the week?

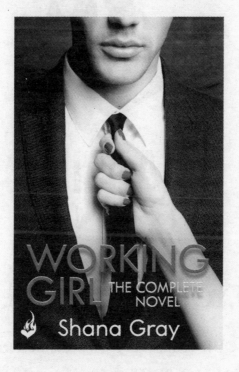

Available now from

HEADLINE
ETERNAL

FIND YOUR HEART'S DESIRE...

VISIT OUR WEBSITE: www.headlineeternal.com

FIND US ON FACEBOOK: facebook.com/eternalromance

CONNECT WITH US ON TWITTER: @eternal_books

FOLLOW US ON INSTAGRAM: @headlineeternal

EMAIL US: eternalromance@headline.co.uk